PART ONE

Novels by Sean Costello

Supernatural Horror
Eden's Eyes
Captain Quad
The Cartoonist

Thrillers
Finders Keepers
Sandman
Here After
Squall
Last Call

Contemporary Fiction
Terminal House

TERMINAL HOUSE

a novel

RED TOWER
original

Red Tower Publications

Red Tower Publications
Sudbury, Ontario
www.seancostello.net

Publisher's Note: This is a work of fiction. Names, characters, places,
and incidents are a product of the author's imagination. Locales and
public names are sometimes used for atmospheric purposes. Any
resemblance to actual people, living or dead, or to businesses, com-
panies, events, institutions, or locales is completely coincidental.

Terminal House / Sean Costello

Print ISBN: 978-0-9731469-9-8
eBook ISBN: 978-0-9731469-8-1

For my mother, Mary Elizabeth, and my grandmother,

Katy-May, dementia victims both.

ONE

Tuesday, May 30, 2028 – *Ottawa*

HE WAS AWARE OF the low thunder of the falls, the cool spray misting his bifocals, the slatted bench on which he sat. But, as so often happened these days, the texture of the moment seemed frayed, his place in it somehow obscure. He'd been coming to this spot at different times for most of his seventy-eight years. What seemed uncertain now was exactly which time this was.

But the day was fine, the spring air balmy, and when he felt this way—no aches or pains, vital inside his skin, almost euphoric—the specter of encroaching Alzheimer's disease seemed much less fearsome than it did when he was rooted in the here and now. Here and now offered only the vagaries of aging: restless sleep interrupted by a grumbling prostate; the unyielding ache of arthritic joints; the subtle restrictions of life in the Eastern Ontario Center for Geriatric Care; and, in spite of the thousands of other fossils housed along with him on the thirty-acre site, a grim and abiding loneliness. Added to this was the growing certainty that in spite of a long and rich professional life, he'd missed the point. Missed it by a mile.

He shifted on the bench now, the hard slats putting his backside to sleep. When he was comfortable again, he noticed his hands. They were old man's hands, liver-spotted and tremulous, and the sight of them startled him. When these disorienting episodes of dementia came, he was seldom an old man. Many times he was little more than a boy.

Maybe it was this place. Hog's Back Falls, where the placid waters of the Rideau River slid under a low bridge to cascade into a rocky gorge. From the time he'd been old enough to make the trip on his own, the falls had been the place he'd come to contemplate life.

He smiled now, remembering other times that had little to do with reflection. Necking in the moonlight. Oh, yeah. His girl saying, "Benjamin Hunter, what *is* that in your pocket?" Playful. Or standing on the spur of rock overlooking the deepest part of the gorge, trying to summon the courage to leap through twenty feet of thin air into the churn of mist and whitewater at the base of the falls. The kids called it The Funnel, a reputedly bottomless chasm with downward-spiraling currents you had to swim like hell against if you wanted to live to tell about it. He never had found the guts.

Slipping deeper into his disease, Ben recalled another trip to the falls, this one decades ago with his pal Ed Quinn—but had it really been all those years ago? Or was it happening now, in this oddly skewed moment? Because he could *smell* the Brylcreem on Quinn now, gobs of it plastering the guy's ginger locks to his skull...gangly, awkward Quinn, with his Coke-bottle glasses, teenage wisp of moustache, and that perpetual glint of mischief in his eyes. They'd biked here from Hillcrest High on their lunch break, thinking they might ditch the rest of the day. History and phys-ed this afternoon, sheer torture, and it was such a beautiful day, spring coming early this year.

Leave it to Quinn to screw things up.

Now Ben heard himself say, "Quinn, you mental case," and he turned away, in the hope that ignoring the wildman would make him stop. He'd only taken his eyes off the guy for a second, and now Quinn was hanging out there on the wrong side of the fence bordering the gorge, gloved fingers clutching the chain-link, feet dangling over The Funnel, the water beneath him freezing on this sunny May afternoon. Christ, there were chunks of ice the size of suitcases tumbling past down there.

Ben said, "C'mon, man, let's head back," and turned to see the fingers of Quinn's fleece-lined gloves still gripping the chain-link—only Quinn was no longer in them. Quinn was nowhere in sight.

"Oh, shit."

Ben sprinted to the end of the fence, pivoted out onto the crumbly ledge and saw his friend down there, clutching the slippery rock-face, the current dragging him under—

"Doctor Hunter, *there* you are."

Squinting against the sun, Ben looked up into a tiny woman's face. A familiar face, smiling down at him the way a teacher might smile at an errant grade-schooler. Somehow, he knew Quinn was going to make it—but still, he had to get to him. He said, "Sister Mary Grace, call an ambulance," and watched the woman's expression turn to one of patient understanding.

"Daydreaming again, Ben?"

He shifted his gaze to the fence. No gloves in the chain-link. Different fence. A cluster of high-rise condos where the Shell station used to be. He'd called the ambulance from there himself...

Ben closed his eyes, past and present swapping places in his mind, the sensation akin to being trapped inside a revolving door for a few brisk rotations before stumbling out the other side.

Looking again at the woman's face, Ben said, "Yeah, Sister, I guess I was." He smiled, trying to mask his bewilderment. "What can I do for you?"

The nun tapped her wristwatch. "Your speech, Ben. Your *speech*. It's in ten minutes. I've been all over the grounds looking for you. And you with no coat. You're going to catch your death out here."

"Right, my speech." As one of the Geriatric Center's founding fathers, now a resident, he'd been asked to say a few words at today's twenty-fifth anniversary celebration.

"Come on," the nun said, reaching for his hand. "I'll help you up."

Ben Hunter got to his feet, letting the nun help him, his knees popping in protest.

How long had he been sitting out here?

Christ, the speech. He hadn't even prepared one. That explained the suit he was wearing, at least.

He glanced over the edge into the roiling falls, flashing again on Quinn, The Funnel swallowing him whole. The son of a bitch had made it out on his own, in spite of Ben's reckless attempts to save him, bobbing up a half-mile downstream with ice in his hair and downy moustache, clinging to a sapling on the flooded bank. Three busted ribs, his glasses, shoes, socks, jean jacket, watch and wallet all gone. Crazy bastard. A couple of guys from a road crew had hauled him up the embankment with a rope.

That had been sixty years ago.

Yet the smell of Brylcreem still lingered in his nostrils.

God help me.

Ben shivered, out of his sheltered niche now, the wind cutting through him in spite of the end-of-May sunshine. That, at least, felt real.

"Come on," the sister said. "If we hustle we can just make it."

* * *

Sean Costello

By the time they reached the gated entrance to the Geriatric Center, a hike of a hundred yards across manicured grounds, Ben had begun to feel more limber, and he shrugged off the nun's supporting grip on his arm.

No matter how many times he viewed the Center from this vantage, he always felt a sense of pride: the lavish admin building in the foreground, with its pillared portico and reflective glass façade; the adjoining twin high-rise condos, reserved for clients capable of independent living; the acute- and chronic-care hospitals, just visible through a stand of budding maples; and beyond that, the Euthanasia Foundation. In his younger days as medical director of the original site—the gloomy husk of the old St. Joseph's Hospital—he'd lobbied hard for the gorgeous tract of riverside land upon which the Center now stood. It had been a heated battle, one he'd come within an ace of losing to a billionaire developer planning to bulldoze it flat and turn it into a shopping mall. He'd called in a ton of favors to help make this place a reality. And whatever regrets he might be harboring now about the way he'd spent his adult life, his role in the creation of the Eastern Ontario Center for Geriatric Care was not among them.

Sister Mary Grace took his arm again. "Come on, Ben," she said. "You're on in two minutes."

*　*　*

14

Clifford Hicks, CEO of the Center, was just finishing up, mouthing platitudes to the attending heavyweights, cordoned off from the rest in a corral of red-velvet rope at the front of the auditorium: the prime minister and his entourage; the mayor and her gang; the big-money sponsors with support staff hovering, topping-up refreshments; the press in a cluster outside the rope.

In a changing world, Ben thought, feeling lucid now and more than a little irritated, *some things never change*.

Sister Mary Grace tugged him along the left-hand aisle, past curving rows of plush burgundy seats, occupied now by residents able to attend. No support staff here, save a few near the back, assisting those confined to wheelchairs. No refreshments, either.

Hicks, CEO for the past fourteen years and a man Ben quietly despised, glanced his way as he climbed onstage and took a seat next to a fellow speaker. The men had locked horns from the outset: Ben, in his role as Medical Director, feeling Hicks was wrong for the job, more interested in politics than sound patient care; and Hicks, a gifted manipulator, hamstringing Ben's every innovation with cries of cost, cost, cost. The lobby alone, uncountable thousands' worth of brass, marble, and stainless steel, could have financed Ben's most extravagant treatment notions a dozen times over. He could still hear the man's stock justification for streaming funds away from medical development: *"When families bring their loved ones here, Doctor Hunter, they need to see this kind of opulence, this kind of confidence."*

Ben said, "My ass," and the woman seated next to him bugged her eyes, saying, "Pardon me?"

Ben tried to shape a reply, but for once Hicks saved him, looking his way now with that shit-eating grin on his face, saying his name into the microphone.

" —introduce Doctor Benjamin Hunter, former Medical Director, now a proud resident of the grand facility he helped pioneer. I asked Ben to say a few words today because I could think of no one better qualified to add such a sweeping perspective to our ongoing efforts here at the Center, both from an historic point of view and, more recently, as an actual client." Hicks extended an open hand. "Doctor Hunter?"

With a quick prayer for steadiness, Ben took the podium. Applause chattered through the large gathering, one white head popping up and shouting, "Ben-*ji*."

Ben chuckled, saying, "Sit down, Quinn, you jackass. I was just thinking about you."

As he waited for the audience to settle, he noticed the big anniversary banner at the rear of the auditorium: *2003-2028. TWENTY-FIVE YEARS OF CARING FOR OUR ELDERLY.*

"God save us," Ben said into a silence that might have lasted longer than he realized. "A quarter century already." He glanced at the crowd, as if seeing it for the first time. "But my, what a quarter century it's been.

"Two-thousand-three. Year of the gene. The human genome mapped and sequenced. The lid on a huge can of worms. Human cloning. Genetically engineered embryos—designer babies. Sex reduced to the status of rec-reation."

"What's wrong with that?" some old guy hollered, getting a few laughs.

"I'm not saying there's anything wrong with it," Ben said. "Look at the array of drugs we have now to keep the lead in our pencils." Behind him, the CEO cleared his throat, a sharp, intrusive sound. "And if the drugs don't cut it, look at the work the Japanese are doing with tissue preparations. Ten years from now, we'll all be able to grow a *new* one, like a salamander's tail. And chances are, most of us'll still be around to see that day. Have a look at our life expectancies: forty-seven in the year nineteen-hundred; seventy-six at the turn of the century; now, it's nothing to be spooning up Pablum at age one hundred."

"Don't get me started on the menu around here," someone shouted—sounded like Quinn again—and a few more laughs tinkled through the big room.

Ben said, "I remember reading an article back in the nineties that predicted the doubling of the elderly population by the year twenty-twenty-five. That informed forecast fell shy by twenty-three percent. We baby boomers turned out to be a tenacious lot. The article also predicted that in the same time period, the number of people suffering from dementia would rise from four million to eight million in the U.S. alone. Enter broad-spectrum anti-aggregates in twenty-seventeen— Alzheimer's all but vanquished in a single stroke, a half-dozen variants of the disease thrown in for good measure."

Quinn again: "And we've got you to thank for that, Doc."

"Well, that's not entirely true now is it, Ed," Ben said. "I was only one member of a very large team." The irony was, he couldn't take the drug himself. He was deadly allergic.

A few photographers swept into the orchestra pit now, flash-glares blinding Ben for a moment. When his vision cleared, he said, "And what about cancer? The great and fearsome slayer of the twentieth century, on the ropes in the twenty-first. Matrix metaloproteinase inhibitors, anti-cancer vaccines, the p53 gene. All gifts of the past decade.

"And the new stuff coming down the pike every month? Pure science fiction twenty-five years ago. Nanotechnology, neural stem cells, *brain* transplants less than a decade away—though I prefer to think of that particular notion as a body transplant.

"But here's the rub, folks. We are deep in the maze of technology now, a maze from which there is no longer any escape. We passed that point five years ago with the extinction of the manta ray and the decimation of the Great Barrier Reef. Egress blocked by progress. Fortunately for us 'clients'"—he glanced at the CEO, tipping him a wry wink—"most of the benefits fall to us, the residents of this fine institution. Here we live in a modern, self-sustaining community. We want for nothing—apart, perhaps, from any sense of individuality or personal freedom. We have the drugs—" He heard his friend Vince Wilder out there saying, "Right on, Doc," but chose to ignore him. Hicks was on his feet now, approaching the podium. "We have the malls and the restaurants, the physiotherapy clinics and the bike paths, the rec center and the greenhouses, and a couple of modern hospitals should we fall ill. And when it all becomes too much for us, as it sometimes will, we have the Euthanasia Foundation, something I helped realize and design. My baby, if you will. As a physician, I saw it as an answer to the kind of suffering that *has* no other answer, save the whims of the gods. Today, as a member of this great community of the aged, I see it in much the same light." He glanced at Hicks, crowding the podium now, and said, "It's the administration of the thing I—"

Hicks made a slicing gesture and the mic went dead, the rest of Ben's sentence "—take issue with," reaching only Hicks's ears. Nudging Ben aside, the CEO bent to the mic and said, "I hate to interrupt," into a live feed. "But we really must press on. Thank you, Doctor Hunter, for that insightful overview."

Now Ben was being led offstage, shielded from the press by silent men clad in black, ushered into a back hall, the door slammed shut behind him.

To hell with it anyway, he thought, tugging on the handle of the metal door, locked now from the opposite side. If he had a point, he'd forgotten what it was. He was hungry now, and it was a long walk to the buffet from back here.

* * *

She approached him in the lobby, a slender girl of no more than eighteen, her support-staff uniform a half-size too big for her. She wore her sandy hair long, a stylish frame for an oval face that transformed when their eyes met, a smile of such unreserved brightness blooming on it Ben felt his heart stumble in his chest.

"Doctor Hunter?" the girl said, sinking to one knee next to the wingchair he was seated in. She was long-limbed and olive-skinned, green eyes flecked with gold, teeth a startling white against the pink of her gums. She exuded cleanliness and youthful vitality and Ben felt shaken by her attention.

He said, "Yes, I'm Ben Hunter. Pardon me for staring, but you reminded me of someone just now."

"Really?" the girl said. "Who?"

Ben was uncomfortable now, long-repressed memories coming in a deluge, muddied by time and regret and the distortions of dementia. "Doesn't matter," he said. "It was a long time ago." It was hard to look into those shining eyes. Hard to stay grounded. "Is there something I can do for you?"

The girl's expression darkened, a worry line creasing her brow. She said, "I heard your speech in there, and I was hoping we could talk."

Ben chuckled, regaining a measure of composure. "Not much of a speech, I'm afraid. More of a rant, really." He indicated the chair next to his. "Why don't you join me? I'd love the company."

Moving with quiet grace, the girl sat primly with her legs crossed and her hands folded in her lap. She said, "I'm Roxanne Austen," and that smile blossomed again. "Call me anything but Roxie."

"Hi, Roxanne, I'm Ben. Call me anything but Doctor."

That got a giggle out of her.

He said, "So what is it you'd like to discuss?"

She hesitated now, glancing at the exit, and Ben got to his feet, instinct telling him privacy was in order. The lobby was noisy and congested, the amplified voice of whoever was speaking in the auditorium adding an echoey backbeat to the confusion.

He said, "Feel like some fresh air?"

Roxanne stood, saying, "You read my mind. It's a bit chilly out, though. Should you grab a jacket?"

"No need. We'll wander down to the solar array. Nice and cozy down there." He offered his arm and Roxanne took it.

And as they made their way out into spring sunshine, Ben felt an almost forgotten excitement, one he hadn't experienced in a very long time.

* * *

They followed the footpath along the river in sun-dappled shadow, a double row of scotch pines screening them from the worst of the wind. Past the sewage treatment dome, a hi-tech marsh where specialized plants and microbes purified waste-water for eventual reuse. Past the open agricultural plots, already tilled, black soil ready for the spring planting, only days away now. To the solar field, a two-acre grid of copper-colored panels embedded in concrete, silently tracking the sun. The warmth down here could be felt from fifty yards away.

They chatted comfortably as they walked, Ben telling her he'd retired from full-time practice at the age of six-ty-eight, then moved in here, a ninth-floor apartment with a view of the falls. Roxanne said she'd finished high school the previous spring, then taken a year off to work at the Center and bank some tuition money. She said she'd been accepted into the environmental studies program at Dalhousie University, and would be starting classes in the fall.

Ben said, "Halifax, huh? Why so far away?"

"They've got the best program in the country."

"Make's sense. Ever been there?"

"Not yet. But I hear it's beautiful."

"It certainly is. I did some subspecialty training there in the eighties. Loved the place."

They came to a shaded bench and Roxanne sat down, that worry line etched in her brow again. Ben sat next to her, thinking this was as good a place as any.

She was clutching the armrest now, bracing herself for what she had to say. Ben had an idea what was com-ing, but when she looked at him, the sun minting gold in her eyes, he experienced another of those vexing dis-locations, the river flowing deep and steely in the near distance, the sun warm on his face, no sense of his aged self and this lovely young woman holding his gaze with such openness and trust...

"It's about my grandfather," she said, the words barely out before her eyes filled with tears and she hid her face in her hair.

Ben said, "Aw, sweetie, come here," and held his arms out to her.

Roxanne leaned into his embrace saying, "I'm sorry," and Ben patted her on the back, hushing her, telling her it was okay.

She let it come now, the force of her upset rooting Ben firmly in the here and now, his back beginning to ache from the weight of her against him, a headache creeping up the back of his neck to clutch his skull.

She collected herself slowly, apologizing again as she pulled away. Sniffling, she dug a tissue out of her uniform pocket and used it to dry her eyes.

Ben was in no hurry, feeling a welcome contentment in spite of the girl's upset. All his adult life he'd felt pulled by outside forces, so unable to just *be* that he'd eventually stopped noticing, coming to think of that driven feeling as normal. But now, as at certain times in the distant past, nothing tugged at him. Here he was, and here he was glad to be.

There was something so familiar about this girl...

She said, "I should start by telling you I was raised by my grandparents. My parents separated before I was born, and my mother died when I was two." She gave a blubbery little laugh. "Sounds like the plot of a really bad soap opera." Ben said it sounded like a bum deal.

Nodding, Roxanne said, "I've never met my father, and I have no clear memory of my mother, so I've always thought of my grandparents as my mom and dad.

"Gramps had a stroke about a year ago. A massive one. Gram cared for him at home for a while, but it was too much." She regarded him with the wounded eyes of a child. "He was so full of fun, and active. Nobody believed he was almost eighty. We used to take long walks together, and he'd tell me about all kinds of things. It was so hard to see his mind just...shut down like that, as if someone had pulled the plug."

Ben knew exactly what she was talking about, had seen it hundreds of times in his geriatric practice. But she needed an ear right now, not an old physician's platitudes.

She said, "It's hopeless now. He just lies there. Fading. Losing weight. He barely even looks like himself anymore. They sponge bathe him and feed him through that tube in his belly. But he's not there. My grandmother's at the end of her rope."

Roxanne brushed away a final tear, and Ben could see her tapping into a vein of steel in her character, a sudden set in her jaw that was again eerily familiar.

"She wants it to end," Roxanne said. "But it won't. So she wants to end it."

"But she wants your consent."

"Yes. She wants my consent."

This was no child's gaze Ben felt on him now. This was the probing scrutiny of a young adult faced with the toughest decision of her life, and it galvanized him, appealing for his most considered judgment before the plea was even shaped into words.

She said, "In your speech you said you saw euthanasia as an answer to the kind of suffering that has no other answer. And even though I have no idea why, I got the feeling you could help me make the right decision."

Ben looked away from her now, feeling his age like never before. He already knew what he was going to say. He merely wanted a moment to assure himself the situation was real and he was fully engaged in it.

Then he said, "Please don't think I'm being glib when I say this, Roxanne, but in my experience, here's what it always boils down to: What would your grandfather want? You described him as an active, loving, intelligent man. If he could see himself now, even for an instant, and could then convey his wishes to you, what do you think he would say?"

And even as he said it, Ben could see the decision framing itself behind the girl's eyes. There was no science to a situation like this. No prevailing medical stance. Life was a finite thing. It had a beginning and it had an end, both of which were most fittingly determined by Nature. It was only now, in this age of power of attorney and informed consent, that such a burden of decision could be placed so squarely on the shoulders of someone so young.

In the woeful silence that now spun out, it was all Ben could do to hold his tongue, the temptation to make the decision for her almost overpowering. A part of him felt he was cheating her by not having a better answer—

for, in fact, answering her question with another question. But he'd been in this position many times in his professional life, and knew the final word had to come from family. All he could do was set the stage, and he'd already done that here.

So he waited.

A black squirrel darted across the lawn and Roxanne raised her eyes to watch it go. It stopped at the edge of the footpath twenty yards away and rose up on its haunches, bushy tail twitching. Roxanne said, "My grandfather says they do that when they're alarmed," and a guy decked out like a Tour de France competitor whizzed past on a racing bike, sending the squirrel scampering back the way it had come.

Roxanne watched the rodent leap onto the trunk of a sprawling oak and clamber out of sight. Then she stood, putting her hand out to help Ben to his feet. "I should be heading back," she said, maintaining her grip on Ben's hand when propriety and mild embarrassment bade him let go. They returned to the Center that way, hands linked in comfortable silence.

* * *

By the time they got back to the admin building the morning's festivities had come to an end, the press vans and limos already gone. Only the cleaning staff remained, picking up after the revelers.

In the lobby, Roxanne hugged Ben and thanked him for his help. She said her grandmother had an appointment with a counselor in the morning, and told him she planned to attend.

As she turned to leave, Ben said if she wanted to discuss it more before the meeting to give him a call...but he could see she'd already made up her mind. She nodded, thanked him again, and left.

Watching her go, Ben felt suddenly drained. It was as if a fresh, sunny day had been eclipsed by despair, and he only stood there, no idea what he should do next. Being in the girl's presence had awakened a long-forgotten sense of purpose, and an even longer-lost feeling of connection, sensations he became aware of only in her absence. And in this moment, with all of that obliterated, a dark part of him felt this might be as good a time as any to curl up and die.

But in spite of having made a career out of death and dying, Ben was terrified of facing his own certain end. Since the Alzheimer's diagnosis eight months ago, he'd been hosting an almost nonstop dialogue in his head, an obsessive turning-over of what he saw as his only options: euthanasia, or the inexpressible horror of dementia. The object of this debate was always the same: Which of these options frightened him most? It was a close race.

Pride—the first deadly sin—had him leaning toward euthanasia. He'd seen enough vibrant, fiercely-intelligent human beings take that slow slide into oblivion to last a lifetime. And the prospect of being randomly disassembled like that, neuron by neuron until there was nothing left but a shitting, gawking, drooling husk resembling a man—*that* was the stuff of nightmares. Viewed in this light, euthanasia seemed the best solution.

But that meant lying on a padded table in one of the euthanasia suites and baring his arm to an expressionless technician, feeling that bright stab of pain as the needle pierced the plump vein at his elbow.

That meant Death by clear-headed decision.

There *was* a third option, and he was prepared for it. In case the disease claimed him before he made up his mind, he'd given Power of Attorney to a trusted colleague, along with a detailed living will. He would've preferred a family member, but his childless brother had died of a heart attack in his forties, and Ben had never married. Either way, the upshot was the same: if the disease got the better of him before he decided, the plan was immediate euthanasia.

Sometimes this third option seemed the most feasible. Once the true decline began, he could hope for a rapid course into insensibility, followed by a painless death by injection.

But he'd seen many Alzheimer's victims regress at the end into a twisted version of childhood, heard them weeping in the night and calling for their mommies.

What if that withered child was somehow aware? Unable to express itself, yet subject to the same paralyzing breed of terror only a child can experience?

What if *he* became that child and they put him on the table and he was aware but unable to let them know?

And round and round…

Ben thought, *Jesus.*

Snapping him out of this dark reverie, his pal Vince Wilder strode up to him now, his expression, as always, full of mischief and cunning.

"Hey, Doc," the old hippie said. "Why so glum?"

"Hey, Wilder. Just...tired."

"Tired, huh?" He took Ben's arm and hustled him outside. "I've got just the thing."

At the end of the walkway Wilder turned right, heading for the greenhouses. Too worn out to object, Ben followed.

* * *

During his teens and early twenties, Ben Hunter had been part of a tight circle of friends that included Ed Quinn, Ray Gale, and Vince Wilder. A few other guys had drifted in and out at different times, but had never fit as comfortably as the original four.

In those days, Quinn had been a reckless dirt bike jockey and perpetual class clown, always in trouble of one kind or another and always keen to take on a dare. It got so the others had to be careful what they said around the guy, because there were many times some casual comment led to situations in which Quinn risked incarceration, serious injury or worse just to impress his buddies. Sweet guy, Quinn, but more than a little crazy. In his mid-twenties, he'd moved north to Moose Factory, where he'd eventually married, fathered three strong boys and become mayor of the town. He'd been a resident at the Center for the past five years, since his wife's protracted death from ovarian cancer.

Ray Gale had been Ben's best friend since the third grade, and was the only member of the gang who hadn't yet become a resident of the Center. As sometimes happened with old friends, time, distance, and the demands of daily living had eroded their connection and, regrettably, Ben had lost touch with Ray more than a decade ago. The last time they'd spoken, Ray had said his forty-year marriage had ended, and had hinted that his thoughts had turned to suicide. At the time, Ben had been laboring under monumental pressures of his own, and when he thought about it now, he wondered if he'd simply been unwilling to get involved in his friend's dilemma. Like so many other things of late, though, the details of those days had grown fuzzy. He kept thinking he should give the man a call, see if he could put things right. Maybe it was a guilty conscience that prevented him from reaching out.

Vince Wilder, the final member of the merry quartet, was an imp of a man who'd lived a nomadic life as a hard-rock miner. Vince's capacity for substance abuse was legendary, but as far as anyone could tell, its long-term effects on him were negligible. At seventy-seven, the man still looked as trim and as hale as he had as a teenager. Just a bit of snow on the roof now, dusting those popcorn curls. His ready smile had separated many a woman from her panties, and his love of mischief hadn't diminished an ounce in all the years Ben had known him. Which was why he was more than a little apprehensive about what Wilder had in store for him today.

Now, hustling along the same footpath he'd shared with Roxanne, Ben said, "Slow down, you spry old bastard," and Wilder paused to let him catch up, matching his stride as they resumed their approach to the greenhouses. There were twenty of them in the near distance, ranked like battlefield coffins beyond the solar array, each a hundred feet long and constructed of glass. Using his abundant charm, Wilder had talked his way into the paid position of Greenhouse Supervisor, and only a select few—Ben among them—knew the real reason why. It was all about access.

Ben was just about to ask Wilder what he had in mind when Ed Quinn plodded up behind them, chuffing like a steam engine. Frantically gesturing, he spent the next several seconds trying to suck enough air into his lungs to speak. Then he said, "I've been all over hell's half acre looking for you two." Stung and annoyed, scrambling to keep up as the men started walking again. "All these years we've been friends, you sons of bitches just sneak off on me like that? You both saw me in the auditorium—Hunter, who was that little cutie you were chatting with in the lobby? Kinda put me in mind of Melanie Anderson, remember her?—why wouldn't you dipshits let me know where you were going?"

Stopping in his tracks, Ben thought, *Melanie, of course,* the familiarity he'd felt in Roxanne's presence clicking in his mind with an almost palpable force. It was so clear now, it amazed him he hadn't made the connection right away.

Something in those shining eyes...

He could still hear Quinn bitching, could see the men advancing along the path...but the scene appeared gauzy now, almost transparent, more dreamlike than real.

What *seemed* real now was the teenage girl opening her locker in the hallway in front of him, autumn sunshine from the tall windows at Hillcrest High smoldering in her hair, and it took his breath away, as it had all those years ago, this girl appearing out of nowhere, the most beautiful creature he'd ever seen in her flower-print dress and sensible shoes, stooping in front of her locker to retrieve a knitted bag.

He'd stopped dead in his tracks that day too, the end-of-class rush parting around him like a tide around a pylon. As if sensing his attention, the girl had risen to her full height and glanced his way. And when their eyes met, she'd smiled as warmly and as unabashedly as if they'd known each other forever. Ben had no idea what *he* had done, other than stand there with his mouth hanging open, whatever urgent after-school plans he'd had forgotten in the face of whatever this was. Instead of looking away, the girl had held his gaze and he wanted to *say* something. But the power of speech had abandoned him, and he only stood there, unblinking.

Now she closed her locker and the moment was gone, the girl striding away with quiet grace, her compact bottom shifting wondrously beneath her thin cotton dress. There was another moment as she passed the tall windows, a sunbeam transilluminating her dress, and he could see her legs silhouetted through the wash-faded fabric. Then she was gone, engulfed by the scurrying crowd—

Something...

Ben said, "What?" an animated shape coming into focus in front of him.

"I said snap out of it, you dozy mutt." It was Quinn, pointing down the footpath at Wilder, the man unlocking a greenhouse fifty yards away. Quinn saying, "You look like you saw a ghost," pulling on his arm now, leading him away from the blissful place he'd just been.

In Quinn's bony grasp, Ben remembered lingering by the girl's locker until the hallway cleared, dazzled by her beauty and the smile that had so thoroughly undone him. He'd made regular trips past her locker after that, hoping to repeat the experience, but his timing was always off. He'd drifted by her in the stairwells a few times, but the opportunity to speak to her never presented itself—and even if it had, he wasn't sure he could've framed a sentence. It was Melanie who finally broke the ice, asking him to the Sadie Hawkins dance that November, sparking a love affair that would wax and wane for the next six years.

Feeling that emptiness again, the withering sense that he'd missed the point, Ben followed Quinn to the greenhouse, the man still bitching about his 'friends' leaving him behind.

* * *

The atmosphere in here was thick and humid, and Ben felt his airways tighten with his first breath. He'd been asthmatic as a child, and just lately it seemed that long-absent affliction was trying to gain a fresh foothold. He'd have to bring it up the next time he saw his family doctor, see about getting an inhaler. If he remembered.

Wilder was nowhere in sight, lost in the tidy rows of aeroponic pillars, all manner of fruits, vegetables, and herbs sprouting in lush profusion from the numerous pockets on each eight-foot tower. The system worked without soil, the exposed roots bathed in nutrients stored in a reservoir at the base of each pillar. And the harvest, staggered across twenty greenhouses, was virtually uninterrupted, the yield sizeable enough to provide year-round produce for the Center.

They found Wilder partway up a stepladder at the far end of the structure, pruning buds off a ten-foot marijuana plant, one of about a dozen growing bold as you please in an earthen bed, a prominent label in Wilder's blocky script identifying the plants as *Acapulco Tea*. Ben knew about the man's clandestine horticultural activities, but clearly Quinn did not.

Leaning in to sniff one of the distinctive leaf clusters, Quinn said, "Is this what I think it is?"

Grinning down from his perch, Wilder said, "Indeed it is. And if you say word-one to *any*body about this, Quinn, I will beat you to within an inch of your life."

Quinn snorted laughter and Wilder said, "You think I'm playing?" the grin vanishing.

Quinn shook his head, knowing full well the man was not only capable of carrying out the threat, but had just enough of a mean streak to go through with it. He said, "No worries, man. I'm just surprised. I always assumed you were buying it somewhere." He made a 'my lips are sealed' gesture and Wilder's grin returned, lighting up those dark eyes.

"Cannabis sativa, my fossilized friends," Wilder said. "Finest daytime high on the planet. Uplifting, energizing,"—looking at Ben as he said it—"spacey as hell." And to Quinn: "A sissy like you might even hallucinate on this particular herb." He pointed at an adjacent greenhouse. "In number three over there we've got sativa's kissing cousin, indica, your basic nighttime high. Soothing body buzz. Sleep like the dead on that bad boy. I make tea for the nuns out of the sativa, gets 'em giggling and hiking up their skirts."

Quinn said, "That's a bad habit to get into," and laughed all by himself.

Coming down the ladder now, Wilder said, "The indica mellows out the Parkinsonians. They pay damn good money for it, too."

"Great," Ben said, "I'm hanging out with a drug dealer now."

"The shit's been legal for a decade," Wilder said, holding one of the conical buds under his nose, eyelids drooping as he inhaled the exotic aroma. Then, with that evil grin: "And every now and again, I get paid with something far more interesting than money."

Quinn said, "Let me guess. Blue-rinse hippie chicks with Parkinson's and no teeth."

Wilder laughed. "It's a winning combination."

Ben said, "I've got to get out of this humidity," and the men left the greenhouse, Wilder locking up behind them.

* * *

They found a bench in the shade of a basswood and Wilder rolled a joint, saying, "It's a little damp, but it'll get the job done." He lit up with a lime-green Bic, the ember sparking as he inhaled a double lungful and closed his eyes, stifling a cough to keep the smoke in as long as he could. As he passed the joint to Quinn, the Olympian toke jetted from his nostrils and Wilder laughed his hippie laugh, regarding them with merry eyes shot red from the assault on his lungs. Now Quinn took a hit, losing it in a barking cough and earning a chastising string of profanities from Wilder.

Eyes watering, Quinn took another quick pull, then held the joint out to Ben.

"No thanks," Ben said, raising his hands in a warding-off gesture. "I'd better pass."

Wilder said, "Too good to smoke with your friends?"

"It's not that, it's—"

"It's what? What is it, Benji?"

Quinn held the joint out again, and this time Ben took it, thinking, *Why not?* He hadn't smoked-up since his twenties, having decided once he hit med school it was time to grow up. But it occurred to him now, with the

36

force of revelation, that being a grownup hadn't done him much good.

He thought, *Screw it.*

As he raised the spit-dampened joint to his lips, he glanced along the bench to see Wilder's impish grin, urging him on.

Giggling, Quinn said, "Reefer madness."

Ben closed his eyes and inhaled, his airways instantly objecting, as they had in the muggy atmosphere of the greenhouse. But gradually, as he drew on the joint to the full capacity of his lungs, the urge to expel the smoke diminished, and now he could hear the other two cheering him on. When he opened his eyes he saw Wilder's big hand in his face, the man telling him not to Bogart the damn thing, and Ben handed it over, the sweet smoke bursting from his lungs on a gale of stoned laughter.

* * *

Roxanne drew the curtain around her grandfather's railed bed, one of four in this cramped, chronic-wing room. Now she sat in a chair by the radiator and took his hand, its limp chill making her shiver. As always, part of her hoped for some response: a slight flexion of his fingers, maybe, or a twitch of awareness in his vacant gaze. But, as always, there was none. He only stared into an emptiness that had already claimed everything but his body.

She said, "Hi, Gramps, it's me. I met a man at the anniversary celebration today. A retired doctor. He's a resident here now, but he used to work for the Foundation.

I told him about you, and he said I should base my decision on what I think you'd want. I've already thought about it. A lot." The tears came now, spilling onto their linked hands. "And I know you wouldn't want to live like this...

"Gram's waiting for me to make up my mind...so I've decided to let her go ahead. I wish you could tell me if I'm doing the right thing—"

Roxanne gasped and held her breath, focusing every brain cell on her hand now, reaching deep into nerve memory to determine whether the tiny stirring she'd just felt had come from her own tense muscles—or from her grandfather's hand. A response of some kind? An affirmation?

She said, "Gramps?" and stood to search his face, squeezing his hand now, hopeful. "Gramps?"

But there was nothing.

Deciding she'd imagined it, Roxanne said, "We're meeting with a counselor in the morning. To sign the paperwork. So this one last time, Gramps, if you can— please—let me know if I'm doing the right thing."

A cloud pulled the light from the room and Roxanne released her grandfather's hand, the downy hairs on her arms standing straight up now, an unbidden image piercing her psyche like a hot needle. She imagined the Reaper hovering over the bed like a vulture on a desert thermal...and in that moment, she understood that the man she'd known and loved had long-since abandoned this shell of a body.

Dry-eyed now, she bent to kiss him on the forehead. Then she left his lonely deathbed for the last time. She did not look back.

TWO

AN INSISTENT KNOCKING WOKE Ben Hunter from a dream that had plagued him during his three-year stint as an anesthesiologist. The dream had vanished after he changed specialties, returning to the University of Ottawa at the age of thirty to study Geriatrics, and it surprised him it had cropped up again now, after so many years.

In the dream, he was doing an urgent case in the OR. He never knew what type of procedure it was, the sterile drape blocking his view, but he knew it was critical: blood bags under pressure; vital signs unstable. There was the stress of it, his own racing heartbeat loud in his ears, and now the surgeon saying, "Is he waking up?" just as the patient's arm rose off the arm board. Ben tried to restrain it, but now the *other* arm angled up, snagging the screening drape, and Ben saw the man's knees strike the instrument tray, tipping clamps and retractors onto the floor in a clatter intensified by the screams of the nurses—

The knocking came again, more insistent this time, and Ben sat up, disoriented in his own daylit room, startled to find himself fully dressed.

Then he remembered smoking pot with the boys, and...

But the rest was a blur, his skull feeling like it was filled with sludge now, sitting up like that bringing the feeling on.

Jesus.

That knocking again.

The door. There's someone at the door.

Ben got to his feet, using the edge of the nightstand to steady himself. Raising his voice, he said, "Hold your horses," and padded out to the door.

It was Quinn.

Yawning, Ben said, "What do *you* want?"

Quinn bulled past him into the kitchen saying, "Is that any way to speak to a friend?" He helped himself to a cider, popping the cap with a *Simpsons* bottle opener as he sank onto the couch in the living room. "What do I *want*? I want to know if you're planning on wearing that wrinkled shit to the variety show in—" he set the opener on the coffee table and checked his watch "—forty-six minutes." Still standing by the apartment door, Ben regarded him quizzically, and Quinn said, "The twenty-fifth anniversary celebration? The *variety* show? My goddamn standup comedy debut? Jesus, man, get the *lead* out."

Making himself at home, Quinn turned on the TV—already tuned to CNN, another violent immigrant crisis in Europe—and scanned to the Comedy Channel, saying, "Oh, look, Robin Williams. You know, after he died—Christ, fourteen years ago now?—it was months before I could watch him in anything without bawling like a ninny. Goddamn shame." He looked at Ben, still by the door, and said, "Will you for Christ's sake get ready?"

* * *

In addition to the usual amenities—billiard tables, tennis courts, golf simulators, exercise room—the rec center housed a spacious hall reserved for concerts, weekly dances, and the variety shows the residents sometimes hosted for special occasions. Tonight's program included talent spots showcasing residents and staff, followed by a dance with live music provided by Relic, a house band made up of a rotating roster of residents. Ben played drums for them sometimes, but he wasn't scheduled to perform tonight. He'd put himself through university playing in a bunch of different bands, and he enjoyed keeping up his skills. These days when he played, it was usually in a three-piece outfit modeled after the legendary power trios of the sixties: Hendrix, Cream, giants like that. The other two guys were former classmates from Hillcrest High: Bill Huggins on guitar and vocals, Roy Segree on bass. They only played the classics, and the old hippies ate it up.

Wilder joined them now, sitting next to Ben at the round table Quinn had reserved near the stage.

"Jesus, Wilder," Quinn said, glancing at his watch. "Talk about cutting it close. I go on in three minutes."

Smelling of weed, Wilder said, "I've already heard all your dumb jokes, Quinn. I'm here for the girl group."

Quinn said, "Screw you, man, I've got all *new* dumb jokes," then grabbed the program, saying, "Girl group?"

Half-listening to his friends' banter, Ben spotted Roxanne in her staff uniform, balancing a tray of hors d'oeuvres. His first instinct was to wave her over, but she looked stressed and he decided against it.

Glancing at the act onstage—a pair of eighty-plus jugglers, the tall one holding a handkerchief to his partner's face now, the tenpin the man had just taken in the beak drawing an alarming amount of blood—Ben said, "Tough act to follow, Quinnsy. You know how these animals love blood sport."

Quinn told him to kiss his fragrant arse.

Now the evening's MC toddled up to the mic on a walker, glancing every few seconds at the humiliated jugglers, waiting until they left the stage before introducing Quinn. She got his name wrong, saying, "Next up we have Ed Quaid in his standup comedy debut," and Quinn hopped to his feet saying, "Wish me luck."

Wilder said, "Break a dick," as Quinn climbed onstage, taking over the mic amidst a polite chatter of applause.

Grinning up there now, watching the MC stump her way into the curtains, Quinn said, "Let's hear it for the bleeders—I mean the jugglers," and got a laugh out of the sizeable crowd.

As Quinn introduced himself, Wilder said, "Whatever possessed him to try standup? The man's about as funny as a high colonic."

Ben said, "Jesus, Wilder, give him a chance. What the hell. We should be supporting him."

"Are you still high?"

"About that. You said the stuff was uplifting, ener*giz*ing—your exact words—and I woke up fully dressed on my bed this afternoon with Quinn banging on the front door. I can't remember a thing after that second toke."

Wilder said, "On a good day you can't even remember your name," and grinned.

Ben knew he hadn't said it to be mean, but it stung just the same. Shrugging it off, he turned his attention to Quinn, a goofy look on the man's face up there now as he launched into his first bit.

"True story, folks. A love story, really. Old dude down the hall from me's gotta be eighty-five, has a crush on this dame with Parkinson's and no teeth." He tipped a wink at Wilder. "He's a shy geezer, but finally one night he screws up his courage and invites the lady over for dinner. Well, one thing leads to another, and before you know it they're in the sack together." A few doubting giggles from the crowd now, and Quinn said, "I kid you not. Anyway, afterward, the old guy's not looking very happy, and his new honey says, 'Wally, you don't look very happy,' and Wally says, 'To be honest, Myrt, I feel kind of guilty.' 'Guilty?' says Myrt. 'Whatever for?' And Wally says, 'Well, if I'd known you were still a virgin, I'd've been more gentle.' And Myrt says, 'That's okay, Wally, if I'd known you could still get a hard-on, I'd've taken off my pantyhose.'"

For a long beat, dead silence from the crowd. Then the place erupted in laughter and applause and Quinn said, "Old Wally must've been wondering why her feet were going..." using his hands to pantomime Myrt's feet flapping like the flippers on a seal. Even Wilder busted a gut, giving Quinn a series of bawdy hoots and shrill whistles.

As Quinn took a bow, Ben was startled by a pair of warm hands covering his eyes. Now the hands were withdrawn and Roxanne leaned over his shoulder, hair smelling of jasmine, radiant smile warming his heart.

She said, "Your friend is really funny."

"Funny looking," Wilder said.

Ben said, "Vince Wilder, this is Roxanne Austen."

Wilder shook her hand. "Pleased to meet you, Roxanne."

"You too, Mister Wilder." Patting Ben's shoulder, she said, "I've only got a minute. Just wanted to come over and say hi."

Ben said, "I'm glad you did."

"I'm here again tomorrow," she said, starting away. "Wanna join me for lunch?"

Ben said, "Cafeteria food? Wouldn't miss it for the world. Dial nine-oh-one-two on a lobby phone and I'll come right down."

Roxanne repeated the number, then scooted away.

Watching her go, Wilder said, "A bit young for you, don't you think?"

Ben glared at him, fists clenched. "Jesus Christ, Wilder, why do you have to smear everything in filth?"

Startled, contrite, Wilder said, "Hey, man, I'm sorry. I didn't mean anything by it."

Red-faced, Ben apologized, startled himself at the vehemence of his reaction. He felt a dull pressure in his skull.

Onstage, Quinn was just wrapping up another gag, something about a guy asking his wife why she never let him know when she was having an orgasm and the wife saying, "'Cause you're never there." Wilder snorted laughter, but the joke fell flat with the rest of the audience.

Looking worried now, Quinn said, "So these two old dudes are alone in the common room playing checkers, and a pair of silver-haired dollies are loitering in the doorway, bitching about how bored they are. All of a sudden, one of them starts getting undressed, saying, 'You know what? I'm gonna streak those two old codgers, see if I can't get a rise out of 'em.' So she does. Toddles right past them, naked as a jaybird. Well the one old lad looks up from the game and says, 'Did you see that?' and the other guy says, 'Yeah. What the hell was she wearing?' And the first guy says, 'I dunno, but it sure needed *iron*ing.'"

That got the place laughing again.

But Ben had lost interest, his eyes scanning the room now, hoping for another glimpse of Roxanne.

* * *

When she got home that night at twelve-thirty, Roxanne was surprised to find her grandmother still awake, reading a novel in Gramps's easy chair with her feet on the ottoman. She looked up as Roxanne came in, saying, "Hi, sweetie. Long day?"

Setting her backpack by the stairs, Roxanne said, "Yeah, Gram, and I'm pooped. It was a good day, though. The formal part in the morning was a bit stiff, but the talent show was a hoot. I'm glad I took the double shift."

Gram said, "You must be so hungry," and started to get up.

Roxanne said, "No, I'm fine," and Gram eased herself back in the chair. "I stuffed myself at the buffet." She sat on the edge of the ottoman now, taking her grandmother's hand. She said, "I stopped in to see Gramps today," and Gram's hand tightened around hers. "To say goodbye."

"Oh, honey. So you've decided?"

Tears flooded Roxanne's eyes and she could only nod. Gram drew her close, cradling her head as she had so often in the past, soothing a skinned knee or a broken heart. She said, "It's the right thing to do, my darling. He was such a good man, I can't bear to think of him suffering."

She stroked Roxanne's hair for a while, humming some nameless tune, and Roxanne felt the guilt melting away. It *was* the right thing to do, and she was glad she'd found someone to help her make the decision.

Sitting up now, she snatched a tissue from the dispenser on the lamp table and said, "I met a neat old guy today. A retired doctor who used to work at the Foundation."

"Mm-hmm?"

"I heard a speech he gave at the ceremony, and I talked to him about it later. He helped me decide."

"Then I'm very grateful to him."

"Me, too," Roxanne said, yawning now. She patted her grandmother's knee and stood. "I'm gonna say goodnight now, Gram. We've got that meeting in the morning and—"

Gram caught her hand as she started away. "Listen, sweetheart. You don't have to go to the meeting. I can handle it on my own. You don't even have to sign the consent. My signature's all they need."

"No. I want to. We're in this together, okay?"

"Okay, hon." She squeezed Roxanne's hand. "You try and get some sleep now."

Roxanne said she would, but she barely slept a wink.

THREE

Wednesday, May 31

RAY GALE, SEVENTY-NINE, strode up to the admissions window in the admin building with a single suitcase in his hand, moving with the same short-statured, barrel-chested vigor he'd possessed as a teenager. Anticipating a tiresome wait, he was pleasantly surprised when the gum-chewing clerk said, "Of course, Mister Gale, we've been expecting you," and slid two white key cards through the half-moon opening in the Plexiglas. "We've got you in the South Tower," she said, pointing to a bank of elevators across the lobby, "which you can access right over there. You're on level twelve, apartment twelve-thirty-three." Smiling, she asked if he'd like a porter to carry his bag and show him to his quarters. Ray thanked the girl and told her he'd be fine.

The ride to level twelve was quick and smooth and Ray stepped out onto plush teal carpet, a sign on the facing wall pointing him left toward his new digs. Moving along the narrow corridor, he thought about who he should visit first. He knew his old high school buddies were all residents here now, and he wanted to hang out with each of them in turn. But he decided to see Ben first. They would have the most to talk about, and he wanted to get the more awkward bits out of the way as quickly as he could. There were fences that needed mending. Then he had a huge favor to ask the man.

The door to 1233 opened with a sigh, the air inside hot and stale, and Ray was annoyed to find the windows all sealed. *Probably afraid of suicides*, he thought, a concept he'd brushed shoulders with more than once in the past. He found a thermostat and adjusted it from 72° to 64°. There was an immediate rush of cool air from a ceiling vent and Ray thought, *Okay, good.*

The apartment was small but conveniently laid out, a narrow kitchenette opening onto a combined living-dining area, with a single bedroom and bath branching off a short corridor. After living in fifteen-hundred square feet of bungalow for the past ten years, it was going to take some getting used to. But, he reminded himself, he wouldn't be staying very long.

A familiar spike of pain ambushed him now, taking him in the lower back, and within seconds he was tacky with sweat. He lowered himself onto the edge of the bed and fished a couple of pain pills out of his suitcase.

Grimacing, he dry-swallowed the pills and leaned forward to relieve the spasm.

Once the pain backed off, he hoisted the suitcase onto the bed, thinking how sobering it was that seventy-nine years of life could be compressed into a single piece of luggage.

Then he called reception and got Ben's apartment number.

* * *

When the knock came on his door at 9:20 that morning, Ben assumed it was Quinn. The man could be a real nuisance, always with some hare-brained scheme that involved either spending Ben's money or breaking a bunch of the Center's ironclad rules. Or both.

But in that first instant as he opened the door, Ben believed he was experiencing another of those jarring dislocations. Because instead of Quinn, his best friend Ray was standing there in faded jeans and a black T-shirt, grinning through his perpetual horseshoe moustache.

Still unsure the man was real, Ben said, "Stingray?" and Ray said "Beanpole?" the way they'd greeted each other since they were kids.

It was *Ray* all right, but a much older version than Ben remembered. The usually jet-black moustache was snow-white now, the male-pattern fringe of hair the man had always so meticulously coiffed almost gone, only a few thin wisps left, also snow-white.

Ben stood frozen for a long moment. Then Ray pulled him into a huge bear hug and Ben smelled his cologne — always *Old Spice* and always too much — and felt the man's bristly cheek against his own.

Tears filming his eyes, Ben said, "Ray?"

"None other," Ray said, nudging him out to arm's length now, looking him up and down. "How *are* you, man?"

"Much better now that I know you're real," Ben said, moving out of the doorway. "Come in. Jesus, man, come on *in*."

Noticing Ben's wet eyes as he stepped inside, Ray said, "Are you crying?"

"Maybe a little."

Grinning, Ray said, "I always said you'd make a nice little girl," and it was like they'd last seen each other only yesterday.

Without asking, Ben fetched a beer for each of them, saying, "To hell with it. The sun's over the yardarm somewhere on the planet."

He sat next to Ray on the couch, noticing only now a grayness under the man's usually robust complexion, and a startling loss of muscle mass, most remarkably between the bones of his hands. Ray had labored hard with those hands his entire life, and had always had the grip-strength of a vice.

Sipping beer in this comfortable silence between friends, Ben admonished himself for donning his doctor hat within minutes of Ray's surprise visit, reminding himself the man was a decade older than the last time he'd seen him. He thought, *Time takes its toll,* and decided to quit being such a worry wart.

Ray took a long pull on his beer, bugging his blue eyes at Ben, making him grin. Growing up together, Ray had always been the funny one, Ben the more serious of the two. Looking at Ray now, acting the fool, Ben recalled occasions in their teens he'd literally had to beg the guy to stop screwing around—usually after they'd smoked a chunk of hash—certain if he didn't, the outcome would be the first fatality from uncontrollable laughter in the history of man.

God, it was good to see him again.

They chatted a while, small talk and nonsense mostly, exchanging a few rude jokes they'd heard. Then Ben asked Ray what had prompted his visit after so many years.

Visit?" Ray said, laughing. "You're not getting rid of me that easily, Benji. I'm your goddamn new neighbor."

Delighted, Ben got teary-eyed again, telling Ray how much he was going to love it here, promising a VIP tour. They talked about how much fun it was going to be to sneak up on those other two happy assholes, and Ben spilled the beans about Wilder's covert horticultural activities.

The mood grew somber after that, and Ben said, "About the last time we spoke..."

Ray raised a hand. "Put it out of your mind, okay? I was in a dark place back then, Angie threatening to leave me every five minutes. But I knew you were hip-deep in your own shit at the time, and I realized only

later how selfish it was to lay all that crap on you then."
Ben tried to interject and Ray said, "Please, man, just
listen. All that talk of suicide? I thought about it. I really
did. Had the shotgun in my *hand* one night." He
laughed. "But you know what stopped me?" Ben shook
his head. "A Cheech and Chong movie. *Up in Smoke.*
Can you believe it? It was on the tube, and I'm sitting
there on Angie's precious Lexington salon sofa—she
was out shopping for matching end tables with money
we didn't have—hoping I'd get brains all over her figured damask draperies, and there's that low-rider coming down the highway with smoke billowing out the
windows, and I started to laugh—like you used to when
you thought you were gonna *die* from laughter, remember?" Ben told him he'd just been thinking about that
and Ray said, "I laughed and laughed, and when Angie
got back an hour later, I was *still* laughing, laughing so
hard I puked all over her vintage Persian rug. I laughed
all the way to the loony bin.

"All this to say…I was clinically depressed. That's all.
Nothing you could've done about it. Nothing any
amount of talking about it could've done. I was in a
locked ward for three months. Psychiatrists, ECT, experimental drugs. The whole nine yards.

"But in the end, this cute little gray-haired shrink lady comes in and writes me a prescription for a new anti-
depressant. Then she tells me to leave my wife. Now get
this. She writes her phone number on the back of the
script and tells me, after I leave my wife to give her a
call."

Ben was grinning now. "So did you?"

"Damn straight I did," Ray said, pausing to drain his beer. "Left the wife, the house, the car and the debt and moved in with the little shrink lady."

"You didn't."

"Scout's honor. Happiest six years of my life."

Ben said, "Six years? But that was a decade ago. What...?"

"Bella got cancer and died," Ray said. "Bella was what I called her. I have no idea why. Her real name was Claire Wedgerfield. Sometimes I called her 'Wedgie'. She preferred 'Bella'. Had it tattooed on the back of her neck."

Now Ray's eyes were wet, but Ben knew better than to say anything about it. What he did say was, "Jesus, I've missed a lot."

Smiling, Ray said, "Indeed you have, my friend." He cuffed the tears from his eyes and said, "Now who do I have to blow to get another beer?"

Ben said, "That'd be me," falling easily into the adolescent banter that had always been their way, having fun with it.

He opened the fridge and shouted, "I'm out of beer. Cider okay?"

"What kind you got?"

"Strongbow. British Dry."

"You realize only a pansy'd have that shit in his fridge."

Ben chuckled. "You want one or not?"

"Bring it on."

Ben tucked one bottle under his arm and tried to twist the cap off the other, then remembered Strongbow didn't have twist-off caps. He set the bottles on the counter and opened the utensil drawer, annoyed to discover the talking *Simpsons* bottle opener a friend had given him was missing. His annoyance flared to rage and he ran the drawer shut so hard the maple front-plate jumped its attachments, striking him on the knee before clattering to the floor. He thought, *Quinn*, and roared, "Fucking *klepto*." The bastard was here last night, raiding the fridge like he always did, and he was constantly going on about that opener, saying how much he wanted one. He must've pocketed the damn thing before they left for the variety show—

Someone came into the kitchen from the living room now, a mean-looking bald guy with a bandit's moustache, and Ben grabbed a butcher knife out of the busted drawer and brandished it at him, saying, "Who the fuck are you and how did you get in here?"

The guy raised his hands saying, "Hey, man, quit screwing around. You're going to hurt yourself with that thing."

Was that...?

Ben said, "Ray?" and lowered the knife.

"Who else would it be? Are you kidding me right now? Because it isn't funny."

Ben put the knife on the counter and opened the next drawer over, yanking it out to the stops, then slamming it shut, saying, "Fucking Quinn. That prick. He *stole* my *Simpsons* bottle opener."

Ray said, "What are you talking about?" He pointed into the living room. "It's on the coffee table."

"Bullshit."

"See for yourself."

Ben moved past Ray into the living room, startled when his friend shied away from him.

The opener was on the coffee table.

Ben sagged onto the couch. "But I thought…"

Ray picked up the bright red bottle opener, inadvertently triggering the voice button. Homer said, *"D-oh!"* in a tinny voice and Ray put the opener in Ben's hand. "It's a cheap plastic toy, Benji. You can pick one up at any Dollar Store. And Quinn wouldn't steal a kiss. Look up *honest* in Webster's and you'll find a picture of that fuzzy primate grinning back at you."

"But I thought…"

* * *

Ray sat on the coffee table in front of his friend, forcing him to make eye contact. At first he saw only vacancy, reminding him of his last view of the bedroom he'd shared with Bella, all the furniture and adornments that had made it special sold at auction. Then, gradually, the shine of presence returned to Ben's eyes and Ray said, "What's going on with you, bro? You scared the hell out of me just now."

"What do you mean?"

Ray said, "You gotta be shitting me." Then it dawned. His mother had succumbed to dementia in her eighties, confusion and hair-trigger fury consuming her gentle soul. He stood now, saying, "Come with me."

Ben put the opener on the coffee table and followed Ray into the kitchen, stopping short when he saw the broken drawer, confusion pinching his features. He said, "Did I...?"

Ray nodded. "Jesus Christ, Ben. Are you—?"

"Going insane?"

Ray could see Ben was more or less himself now, and he did what he always did, tried to make light of the situation. "I was going to say batshit crazy, but yeah. Is that what's going on here?"

Ben stared at his feet, embarrassment creeping up red from beneath his collar. "Yeah," he said, barely above a whisper. "That's exactly what's going on."

* * *

Though Ben felt centered now, the details of the past several minutes still lay jumbled in his brain. His last clear memory was of going to the fridge.

But as he surveyed the damage in the kitchen, fragments of those scrambled minutes flashed in his mind like subliminal movie frames: trying to twist the cap off the cider; slamming that drawer; fury overwhelming him...

Jesus. This is bad.

Shaken, he returned to the couch, averting his gaze as Ray sat next to him, shame still burning in his face. Deciding to fess up, he said, "On and off for about a year

58

now, I've been having these…episodes. At first I passed it off to daydreaming or simple absentmindedness. But I worked with the elderly for a very long time, Ray, and I knew full well what was happening had little to do with daydreaming. So I saw a colleague…" He drew a breath and released it. Then he locked eyes with Ray. "It's Alzheimer's, man. Fucking Alzheimer's. Right now it's episodic, worse when I'm tired or stressed. But the disease is progressive. To be perfectly blunt, my brain is shriveling. A nice plump grape becoming a raisin."

"But what about the treatment you discovered, the anti…"

"Anti-aggregates. Aggrecene. You know about that?"

Nodding, Ray said, "Bella told me. Showed me an article in a medical journal. Aren't you on it?"

"You told her about me?"

"Of course."

Ben flashed on the day eight months ago when the treatment he'd helped to develop took a savage turn on him, almost ending his life. He said, "Turns out I'm allergic. Ever heard of anaphylaxis?"

Ray nodded. "I have a cousin allergic to peanuts. Has to carry an EpiPen. She almost died a couple times."

"Well, that's what happened to me." He chuckled, a dry, humorless sound. "How's that for a grim irony."

"Isn't there something else they can try, though? There must be some other way to…"

"Hey, man, I didn't mean to upset you. Most of the time I'm fine." He gave Ray's knee a congenial pat. "And you know what? I'm glad it's out in the open between us—and I'd like to keep it that way, if you don't mind. Between us." Ray gave him a nod. "At least now you'll know what's going on if I say or do something inappropriate."

Ray said, "So what's Quinn's excuse?"

Ben chuckled, feeling better for having leveled with his friend. He said, "My grandmother had the same problem. She was in a seniors' home toward the end, after you moved to Toronto. Most times, like me, she was fine—sharp, funny, proud of her grandson the doctor. But every once in a while, in the middle of a sensible conversation, she'd look off to one side and say something to my long-dead grandfather, like, 'Albert, shut that *god*damn barn door'. Then she'd be fine again. I used to wonder what that was like. Now I know first hand."

"What *is* it like?"

"Actually, it's hard to describe, because short-term memory's the first thing affected. And when I come back from wherever I've been, quite often I can't remember a thing. Much like when you wake up from a dream, the details there and then gone, other things rushing in to take their place. Sometimes I can feel it coming, like a trance or extreme fatigue, the mind wanting to shut down. Or in my case, change channels. And usually all it takes is some external stimulus to snap me out of it, like you confronting me in the kitchen just now. But that's early stages we're talking about, bud. In a matter of weeks, days, even hours, I could go off the deep end and never come back."

Ray was shaking his head. "Jesus, man. You scared the hell out of me. You were *furious*. I've never seen you like that, not in all the years I've known you. And you had no idea who I was."

Ben looked away, frightened now, too. As far as he knew, none of his previous episodes had unleashed the kind of rage it must have taken to destroy that drawer.

God, why can't I remember?

But he knew. Better than most, he knew.

Ben felt the sting of tears, and now Ray's arm around his shoulders, Ray saying, "Hey, buddy, come on. You'll get through this. You're one tough muther, you know it? I've never told you this, but you've always been a hero of mine." He grinned. "The way chicks swarmed around you in the seventies?" Ben snorted laughter. "Getting into medical school. You're a goddamn *doctor*, for Christ's sake. Writing those books. Finding a *cure* for batshit crazy."

Now they both laughed.

Ray said, "The fact you can't take your own medication, that sucks the big one." Ben felt the man's grip tighten around his shoulders. "But you're gonna be *fine*, okay, man? You're gonna be just fine."

Ben knew better, but held his tongue.

They sat in silence for a while, their breathing the only sound. Then Ray said, "If you've got a screwdriver, I can fix that drawer."

* * *

Following a quick tour of the complex, they found Quinn and Wilder sitting at a picnic table in the shade of a chestnut tree, sharing tea and brownies with a small group of nuns, Sister Mary Grace among them. For the first few moments, neither of the grinning idiots recognized Ray, and Ben had to say, "Remember this guy?"

Quinn got it first, squinting behind dirty glasses until he made the connection, and he hooted so vigorously his top denture popped out and landed in his tea. That got the nuns giggling, and Quinn said, "Ray? I'll be *God* damned," with a wet slur, the mild blasphemy earning him the evil eye from Sister Mary Grace. "How long has it been?"

Now Wilder came around the table to shake Ray's hand, telling him it was good to see his ugly ass again, and Ray pulled the man into a stiff hug. Wilder had never been comfortable with displays of affection, but today he allowed it. Barely.

Quinn came next—at six-foot-six, towering over Ray's five-eight—the old softy on the verge of tears. Ray offered his hand and then feinted, pretending to sock the man in the belly. Quinn jackknifed like he'd been gutshot and the nuns shrieked in horror. Ray embraced the man then, pleased to be back with the old gang.

Wilder was already pouring tea from a chrome thermos for the new arrivals, filling a pair of paper cups to the brim with the pale brew.

The men crowded in next to the nuns now, Ben introducing Ray to the sisters, pausing at one incredibly ancient gal—the only one wearing the traditional black-

and-brown penguin suit—to say, "And this is Sister Mary Aloysius. You might remember her from grade school. The principal at Corpus Christi during our checkered tenure there? She of the work detentions and leather strap. If memory serves, you were one of her favorite targets for that good old Christian brand of corporal punishment."

Ray studied the woman's deeply seamed face, disbelief shading to wonder as she peered back at him through John Lennon bifocals, saying, "Raymond Gale. *I* remember you. Always parking that blue and white bicycle of yours on the school lawn."

Shaking his head, Ray leaned away from her to whisper in Ben's ear, "Is it really her?" Grinning, Ben said it was and Ray said, "Jesus Christ, she's got to be a hundred."

"Hundred-and-six."

Glancing at the nun again, Ray said, "Owly bitch still gives me the creeps."

"I heard that, Mr. Gale," Mary Aloysius said. "And don't think I won't take the strap to you right here in front of your juvenile delinquent confederates." The old woman laughed now—revealing the last of her teeth, leaning like yellow tombstones in her ancient mouth—and said to Wilder, "More tea please, Vincent."

Grinning, Wilder said, "Happy to oblige."

* * *

Things loosened up after the nuns left, all of them giddy on Wilder's brownies and tea, marveling as they strolled away at how light and joyful they always felt after sampling the man's wares. Ben was amused and a little astonished at their naiveté—though he got the distinct feeling Mary Aloysius knew exactly what was going on and got a hell of a kick out of it anyway. *A hundred-and-six-year-old stoner.* The thought made him smile.

Sitting here now, listening through a pleasant buzz to his friends' chatter, Ben thought, *I probably shouldn't talk—baked like a hippie two days in a row.* And he realized then, nibbling one of the brownies, he hadn't felt this good in years: his joints no longer felt like they were packed with ground glass; his mental status was sunny and light, none of the usual doom and gloom rattling around in his head; and he felt solidly grounded for the first time in months, with a clear sense of who, where—and *when*—he was. He thought, *Maybe there* is *some benefit to this stuff after all.* Although for decades he'd rejected the notion, believing 'medical marijuana' was simply an excuse for a lot of people to get rich and a lot of other people to get stoned.

Quinn and Wilder took off at twelve o'clock, the munchies hard upon them now, Wilder saying it was mac-and-cheese day in the caf, his favorite. Quinn asked Ray if he wanted to join them, but Ray declined, saying he wasn't hungry and wanted some alone time with Ben.

Watching the men shuffle away, Ray said, "Mutt and Jeff."

Ben laughed. "With all due apologies to the *real* Mutt and Jeff."

Ray said, "I'm glowing. Are you glowing?"

"Like a click beetle."

"Feels like old times."

"That it does."

Fifty feet away on the footpath, Sister Mary Aloysius motored past on a scooter, giving them a wave and a gap-toothed grin.

The men waved back, Ray saying, "Bitch," under his breath. As she rolled out of sight, almost tipping the scooter on a tight corner, Ray said, "What's with the nuns, anyway? There was nothing in the brochure about this being a Catholic facility."

"No, you're right. They're actually residents, but they look after the chapel and do amazing amounts of volunteer work. They're well loved around here."

Ray snorted laughter. "Mostly by Wilder. Funny as hell, seeing them get high without realizing it." He pointed after Mary Aloysius. "Except that evil witch. I'm pretty sure she knows *exactly* what's going on."

"Agreed."

"Ten bucks Wilder's banging her."

Their laughter rose on the spring air, flushing sparrows out of the chestnut branches above their heads.

* * *

That mellow high lingered into the afternoon, the men filling the hours in the breezy shade chatting about old times…how they met in the third grade, the first time they smoked-up, got laid, got in a fist fight, failed a grade, left home, bought a car, almost went to Woodstock, stole a couple of *Playboy* magazines and got caught pulling their pugs—Ben by his mother, Ray by Ben.

Laughing, Ben said, "I seem to remember an *ugly* purple helmet on that thing."

Ray turned beet red, still embarrassed after all these years. "You should learn to knock before you come barging into a guy's bedroom."

To change the subject, Ray came up with the idea of voting on what was the coolest thing they'd ever done together. After much deliberation, they narrowed it down to either setting out to make a coastal run around North America on Ray's 350 Honda, or seeing Led Zeppelin live in 1970. After Ben reminded Ray about their motorcycle jaunt ending in a nasty spill in the Mojave desert—and they compared long-healed patches of road rash—it was decided that seeing Zeppelin in concert was probably the coolest thing *any*one had ever done.

Pensive now, the westering sun beginning to glare-blind him, Ray said, "Those guys were magnificent."

"Indeed they were."

"Robert Plant was a god, man. I remember looking up at him and wondering what it must be like, being that beautiful and *con*fident and uniquely talented, every chick in the place ready to worship your cock. Jesus." Ray laughed, shaking his gleaming head. "The man's jeans were so tight, you could count the wrinkles on his nutsack."

Ben said, "You'd've blown him if he let you."

Ray laughed. "You're the little girl, not me."

They were quiet after that, each man idling in his own mental space, observing the goings-on around them: pigeons and gulls squabbling over bits of stale bread the resident bird lady tossed on the footpath; old folks tooling past on motorized carts or walkers, rheumy eyes focused on an irretrievable past; visitors exiting the Center, relieved as they hustled back to their cars, glad to be free of the sanitized atmosphere of decay that permeated the place.

After a while, Ben suggested they go back inside, saying he was getting sunburned and hungry. But Ray said, "There's one more thing I wanted to talk to you about," his demeanor subdued now. "I need a huge favor."

"Sure, man, whatever you want."

"Let's not get ahead of ourselves, okay? Hear me out before you decide."

"All right."

Ben looked into his friend's eyes now, bracing himself against the dark thing he saw lurking there.

Ray said, "I've got—"

"*There* you are."

Ben turned to see a slender shape coming out of the sun—it was Roxanne—and his concern over what Ray had to say was replaced by joy. Followed instantly by guilt.

"Lunch," he said, feeling the blood rush to his face. "Oh my God, sweetie, I forgot."

But Roxanne was smiling, scooting to sit next to him now, clutching his hand. "That's *fine*, Ben. Please, don't worry about it. I forget things too, all the time."

Ben said, "I...we..." glancing at Ray now, feeling equally guilty about the interruption—clearly his friend had something important to tell him.

But Ray gave him a subtle nod, as if to say, *Don't worry, buddy, we'll come back to this later.* Winking, he said, "Take your foot out of your mouth, you forgetful old fart, and introduce me to your friend."

"Of course," Ben said. "Ray Gale, this is Roxanne Austen. We met yesterday at the anniversary bash. She'll be going into environmental studies at Dalhousie in the fall."

Offering her hand, "Roxanne said, "Hello, Mister Gale, how are you?"

"Not bad for the mileage," Ray said, shaking her hand. "Nice to meet you, Roxanne. And Mister Gale was my dad. Call me Ray." Then to Ben, "Listen, old boy, why don't you two go ahead and visit. I'm gonna head back to the apartment. I haven't even unpacked yet."

Secretly delighted, Ben said, "Are you sure?"

"Yeah, yeah," Ray said, starting away. "I'll catch up to you later."

Ben said, "Okay, Stingray," and Roxanne giggled.

"Later, Beanpole," Ray said, and he was gone.

Ben rose now too, saying, "I feel like such an old fool. I'm so absentminded." Roxanne told him it was no big deal, and Ben said, "It *is* a big deal. I really have to start writing things down." *Then remember I did.* "Let me make it up to you. They've got this chocolate-coated ice cream in the boutique that's to die for. Häagen-Dazs on a stick. Salted caramel. My treat."

Smiling, Roxanne said, "You're on, *Bean*pole."

Blushing again, Ray said, "I was a skinny kid."

* * *

"Wanna walk with these?" Ben said, taking a bite of the delicious treat.

"Sure," Roxanne said, digging in now, too.

And in a reflex that would soon become routine, they bore right along the footpath fronting the admin building, moving toward the solar array, Ben half-wishing she'd take his hand again. But Roxanne was busy devouring her ice cream and Ben chuckled, saying, "Told ya."

"Mmm, these *are* delicious. I can already feel myself getting addicted."

They were quiet now, walking and snacking, and Ben went away for a while, flashing on something as the Euthanasia Foundation came into view, an ornate, donut-shaped building set apart from the main complex on an acre of manicured grounds. For no conscious reason, he turned onto a side path, heading for the building now. It was Roxanne's tentative voice—"Ben, where are we going?"—that snapped him back.

"Nowhere in particular," he said. But he glimpsed a motive skipping through his mind like a flat stone and he hesitated, ashamed and confused by what his ailing brain served up: *You're trying to impress the girl.* As if beyond his volition, he continued moving toward the Foundation, tossing the stick from his ice cream into a waste bin. "I just thought you might like a tour—"

Roxanne grabbed his hand, not companionably this time but roughly, urgently, the rims of her eyelids flashing red.

She said, "I don't want to go in there, okay, Ben? Not ever again."

He glanced at the entrance, not twenty feet away now, but still not close enough for Roxanne to read the inscription on the marble cornerstone: THE BENJAMIN HUNTER BUILDING, ERECTED 2018. He thought, *Why would I want her to see that?* realizing only now what a boneheaded move this was. Her grandfather would soon meet his death in there.

"I'm sorry, Roxanne," he said, glancing at the remains of her ice cream, melting now in the sun, runners of chocolate and vanilla oozing between her fingers. He tugged his hand free of her grip, dug a clean tissue out of his pocket and wrapped it around her hand, apologizing again, saying, "I wasn't thinking."

"That's okay," Roxanne said, tossing the rest of her treat into a waste bin. "Let's just go sit by the falls, okay?"

Ben only nodded.

They made the quarter-mile hike in freighted silence, Roxanne walking a few paces ahead of him now, wiping her fingers with the tissue. Winded and ashamed, Ben did his best to keep up, fearful his ego might have harmed their budding friendship. It had been a juvenile move, wanting her to see his name on that stone, imagining her saying, "Oh, cool, they named the building after you."

Trailing her down the steps to the falls, Ben thought, *Idiot*, not realizing he'd said it aloud until Roxanne said, "What?"

"Oh, just calling myself an idiot," he said, red-faced. "Didn't realize I'd said it out loud."

There was a bench nearby, bolted to a rocky promontory overlooking the falls, and Roxanne took Ben's hand and led him to it.

Sitting next to him now, she said, "I'm the idiot," her frank gaze unnerving him, as it had the day before in the lobby. *So beautiful.* She said, "I'm being such a baby about this. But I can't help it."

He saw tears mist her eyes—and watched her stifle them with the same vein of steel he'd glimpsed the day before.

Lowering her gaze, she said, "I signed the consent this morning."

"Yes, of course. Your appointment with the counselor." He waited for her to say, "I saw the marble stone with your name on it," and thought, *What is* wrong *with you?*

71

She said, "I saw your name on the building—you must be so proud they named it after you—but I'm sorry, Ben, the place gave me the creeps. Sitting with that counselor, and then going on the tour, I kept thinking, 'My Gramps is going to die in here,' and I couldn't wait to get back outside. I couldn't breathe, and..."

Ben said, "Shh, kiddo, shh," and put his arm around her. And in spite of the girl's upset, he felt warm and necessary and real.

She gathered herself quickly, and when she pulled away Ben felt as if a small part of him had been excised, a visceral tug that left him feeling diminished.

He said, "When?"

"Tomorrow morning. Nine o'clock."

Ben thought, *First of the day*, recalling the first client he'd euthanized on opening day, November 26th, 2018, the task falling to him by default. In spite of Medical Assistance in Dying having been legalized two years prior, there had been a huge public outcry that morning, hoards of pro-lifers storming the gates with placards and chants of government-sanctioned genocide. Something about centralizing a process that had been going on peacefully and humanely in hospital rooms, palliative care facilities, and patients' homes for the preceding twenty-four months had lit a righteous fire under the demonstrators, and the situation had quickly escalated into violence and arrests. Watching the action from a third story window, Ben had recalled a similar furor in the early seventies surrounding the legalization of abortion. Thankfully, though, in both instances, the volatility of the situation had diminished over time, only the most rabid detractors refusing to let go. To this day, small, joyless groups of them picketed the Foundation, bobbing their signs and expounding the 'Will of God' to all who would listen. Even changing the name of the process from Medical Assistance in Dying to Voluntary Euthanasia—in an attempt to shift perceived responsibility from the operator to the client in the least offensive manner possible—had failed to mollify them.

Now Ben watched Roxanne smooth out the tissue he'd given her, the thin material stained with chocolate, and use it to dry her eyes, getting a freckle of chocolate on her cheek. Smiling, he wet the ball of his thumb, like his mother used to do, and scrubbed the speck away. Bringing it back to his lips, he said, "Isn't that chocolate to die for?"

Roxanne chuckled and the tension broke with a tiny sigh.

They shifted on the bench now to face the falls, the cascading roar soothing, the occasional breath of mist cool on their faces.

After a while, Roxanne said, "In your speech yesterday—"

"Rant."

"Okay, *rant*. Mister Quinn said we had you to thank for the progress on Alzheimer's disease. What did he mean by that?"

"First of all, hearing anyone call Quinn 'Mister' makes me wanna drop to my knees in hysterics. And once you get to know the man, you'll see he has a tendency to exaggerate."

"Or maybe you're just too modest."

Ben felt himself blushing again, something he believed he'd outgrown decades ago. He said, "You know who Francis Riley is?"

"The billionaire energy guy who orbits the planet in his space shuttle all the time? *That* Francis Riley?" Ben nodded and Roxanne said, "Who doesn't?"

"Well, early in twenty-seventeen, when I was scrambling to fund the Foundation, the man called me out of the blue and said he had a proposition for me. His wife Dawn had just been diagnosed with early-onset Alzheimer's—she was thirty-eight at the time—and Francis was beside himself. He said he'd read about our work with anti-aggregates and knew we were running short on funds. He asked if I thought the drug would work and I told him I was almost certain. So he asked how much we needed to complete the research, and couriered a check to me for twice that amount the next day."

"Wow."

"No kidding. My hand shook holding it. Now here's the thing, Roxanne—and you have to swear you'll never breathe a word of this to anyone. I could go to prison if what I'm about to tell you ever got out, and I'm too old to wind up some hardcore convict's love kitten."

Roxanne giggled, but swore herself to secrecy.

Ben said, "The stage we were at with anti-aggregates at the time, it was going to be at least two years before we got anywhere near human trials, never mind Health

Canada approval. And Riley's wife had already attempted suicide twice during her lucid intervals. So..."

Ben covered his mouth with his hand, a prudent inner voice telling him he was crazy, admitting the commission of a federal crime to a teenager he barely knew.

But before he could say any more, Roxanne said, "I think I know where this is going. And even though I can assure you I'd never repeat a word to anyone, if you don't want to tell me, I'm okay with that. I won't be insulted or anything."

"All right. Let's make a little game of it, then. You tell me where you think it's going and I'll nod or shake my head."

"You started treatment on her right away, without jumping through all the legal hoops."

Ben nodded.

"And it worked?"

"Like a charm. She'll have to stay on the drug the rest of her life, of course, but she's writing children's books now and sits on the board of directors of the Foundation. Riley was so grateful, he wrote another check, this one for the construction of the building. It should be called the Riley Foundation. He cemented-in that hunk of marble with my name on it at the ribbon-cutting ceremony the following year."

Roxanne said, "That's incredible," and leaned in to kiss him on the cheek, her breath warm on his skin. She said, "You're a hero," and Ben felt himself beaming like a sunrise.

* * *

Sitting on the bench with Roxanne, Ben felt his mind begin to tilt, and at some level he knew he was slipping. But he also knew there was nothing he could do about it and so he closed his eyes, letting it come, almost inviting it on this idyllic spring evening, his companion's shoulder warm against his own, no pain in his body now...and when he glanced at Roxanne, she was someone else. Someone from a long time ago. Someone he'd given his heart to in the callow, headlong fashion of the very young, the girl barely sixteen, himself only a year older.

Melanie

It had been sunny that day too, but closer to winter, a bracing chill in the air, the maple they were nestled under losing its leaves in the wind. Ben was holding something in his hand, and he looked at it now—*God, yes*, his grandfather's wedding band, a small treasure his grandmother had given him after the old man passed. He was going to offer it to his girl, ask her to go steady—

A familiar voice now, flat and distant: "What did you say?"

Glancing at his empty palm, Ben said, "Did I say something?"

Roxanne said, "I thought you just asked me to go steady." Smiling, but perplexed.

"Did I? I'm so sorry."

Laughing, Roxanne said, "No need to apologize," and gave his sleeve a playful tug. "It's the best offer I've had in ages."

It was clear she was teasing, but her response unbalanced him, and he looked again at his hands. *Old man's hands.* And while the sight of them should have grounded him, as it had so often in the past, now it only deepened his confusion.

Roxanne said, "You looked like you were daydreaming."

Seeing a way out, Ben said, "Yeah, I do that sometimes." He didn't want to lie to the girl, but he could see little point in telling the truth; he'd done enough of that for one day. He tried to convince himself it was because he didn't want to upset her, but deep down he knew it was pride. Settling for a half-truth, he said, "Old age, I guess. We codgers tend to drift off the rails from time to time."

Roxanne laughed. "*Codgers.* Gram says age is just a state of mind. Gramps was a daydreamer, too. The simple truth is, he just lost track sometimes. It's nothing to be ashamed of."

"What a refreshing way of looking at it."

Roxanne glanced at her watch. "Oh boy, I'd better get rolling. It's my turn to make dinner and Gram's a bear when she gets hungry." She stood. "Wanna walk me to my bike?"

Ben smiled, still a little wobbly. "I'd love to, hon, but I think I'm just going to sit here a while. Watch the sun go down."

Roxanne said okay and bent to give him a peck on the forehead. Then she was gone, trailing a scent of jasmine, leaving a tiny hole in Ben's heart.

* * *

The first hardy mosquitos of the season harried him back to the Center, and Ben mused as he walked that a respectable version of Hell might be an eternity spent in a room swarming with the nasty beggars, each coming back to life after you swatted it flat.

Ray was waiting for him in the lobby, hunched over an old *e*-reader. The reader surprised Ben. During his disillusioned stint as an anesthesiologist, he'd written three novels that got picked up by Random House— he'd gone through a brief Robin Cook phase, thinking he could make a bundle writing medical thrillers and retire to the French Riviera—but Ray had never read them, not even the one Ben had dedicated to him, claiming he lacked the attention span for fiction. Ben ragged him gently about it now, but backed off when he saw the tortured expression on his friend's face.

He sat next to Ray and touched his arm. "Hey, man, are you okay?"

Ray closed the reader. "Yeah, yeah, it's nothing. Just a little back pain. It'll pass."

Ben wasn't convinced, but he knew better than to persist. If Ray didn't want to talk about something, even a beating wouldn't drag it out of him.

"Okay. What are you reading?"

"Stephen Hunter," Ray said. "*Dirty White Boys.* Bella loved the guy." He held up the reader. "She gave me this for Christmas a month before she died. It was already loaded with some insane number of books. Couple thousand, I think." He managed a pained smile. "Yours are in here, too."

"Did you read 'em?"

"Every last one."

"And?"

Ray said, "Hang onto your day job," and laughed.

"Asshole."

"No, man, I loved them. Really. Almost teared up when I saw the dedication in *The Surgeon.* Did you actually *work* with a psycho like that or is he made up?"

"Pure fiction, my brother. Product of a sick mind."

Laughing again, Ray said, "No argument there." He closed the reader and stood. "You up to finishing our chat?"

"You bet."

"Come on then, I'll show you my place."

Ben chuckled. "I'd bet my left nut it looks exactly like *my* place."

Heading for the elevators now, Ray said, "Yeah, but I bet your place doesn't have a chunk of hash the *size* of your left nut in it," and pulled a silly face. Then: "On second thought, maybe the size of *my* left nut, seeing as you don't need a magnifying glass and tweezers to find it."

Ben gave him a playful swat, saying, "Wilder?"

Thumbing the UP button on the call panel now, Ray nodded. "Palmed it to me at the picnic table."

"Goddamn. Getting high for the third time in two days. It's starting to feel like the summer of love all over again."

The elevator arrived and the men stepped aboard. Pressing 12 with a shaky finger, Ray said, "You see anything wrong with that?"

Ben only grinned, feeling like a teenager again.

* * *

Ben said, "Cold as a meat locker in here."

Ray was standing at the Formica countertop in the kitchen, slicing the hash into slivers with a pocket knife, then rolling them into balls the size of a match head.

Watching from the living room, Ben said, "The men in black catch you with that weapon, they'll confiscate it."

"They're welcome to try. Who are the bastards, anyway? Slinking around with clipboards. Bella worked in the hospital system for thirty-five years and she used to tell me, 'Never trust anyone with a clipboard'. What's the story with those guys?"

"Clifford Hicks, the CEO here, calls them his 'Security Team'. I used to ask him, 'Security from what?' Most of them are retired cops or ex-military. Creepy guys. Nobody messes with them, that much I can tell you. When I was medical director, we had a staff of about a dozen guards, overweight retirees looking to make a few extra bucks punching watchclocks. But these guys...I don't know what Hicks was thinking, hiring them. Do something they don't like, they're quick to put their hands on you."

Ray brandished the three-inch blade. "Good way to lose a finger."

"I hear you. But trust me, if you want to hold onto that thing, keep it out of sight."

Ray placed the last ball of hash on a square of tinfoil, then switched on an element on the stovetop. While the element heated, he scouted through the kitchen drawers until he found a couple of stainless steel butter knives, which he inserted tip-first between the coils of the reddening element. Then he motioned for Ben to join him at the stove.

Grinning, Ben said, "Hot knives. Brings back memories."

"Yeah, one in particular. You so baked on Afghani border hash you branded your bottom lip with the knife and didn't even notice."

Ben laughed. "I get dumb as a post on that shit."

"Then prepare to get all-the-way retarded."

Ray handed Ben a plastic drinking straw, picked up one of the knives and dropped a ball of hash onto the glowing tip. The drug ignited, releasing a thin streamer of smoke. Using his free hand, Ray grabbed the second knife and pressed it over the burning chunk, Ben leaning in now to suck an explosion of smoke through the straw. The toke was shockingly harsh and he leaned away from it, straining to hold it in. Ray seized the straw with his teeth and took over, capturing the last curls of smoke before tossing the knives clattering into the sink.

Facing each other now, the men slipped into an old contest—seeing who could hold onto the hit the longest—and, as always, Ray won. Ben told him it was because he never went first and had an unfair advantage, a chest the size of a rain barrel.

Hacking as he ejected the last of the toke, Ben said, "Your 'stache is on fire," and Ray leaned over the sink, blasting cold water over his moustache to douse the tiny flame.

Red-eyed, Ben said, "I love the smell of burning hair in the morning."

Ray said, "Then you must be fucking too fast," and they laughed until Ben almost puked.

* * *

After deciding three hits of Wilder's killer blend was enough, the two old friends retired to the couch. Ben offered to scoot down to his place for a couple of ciders and Ray said maybe later.

Cuffing tears of laughter from his face, Ray said, "It may have been a bit slippery of me, getting you shit-faced before talking about this, but think of it as Irish courage. Considering the favor I'm about to ask, I'm pretty sure you're going to need it."

"You'd better spill now, buddy, okay? You're scaring me a little here."

Ray said, "Harshing your buzz?" making the kind of goofy face that normally would have tipped Ben into spasms of stoned laughter.

But Ben said, "Come on, man. Focus. Let's get whatever this is behind us."

Nodding, averting his bloodshot eyes, Ray said, "I've got cancer." Ben started to say something and Ray said, "It's metastatic, bud. Bone, lung, liver, brain. It's everywhere."

Ben felt slammed, thinking he'd seen it right away, that grayness in his friend's complexion, the loss of muscle mass. He said, "Shit, man, I am so sorry. But listen, it may not be too late. I know specialists here at the Center, total pros. We could—"

"That's not the favor I wanted to ask," Ray said, raising his eyes to meet Ben's now, the redness in them not solely from the hash. He said, "Remember that remake of *The Fly* back in the eighties?"

"Jeff Goldblum."

"Yeah. At one point in the film, he says something that's stuck with me all these years. Because I knew I'd feel the same way if I ever got cancer. I don't remember the exact words, but it went something like, 'I don't want to be just another tumorous bore'. I've been struggling with this thing for over a year now, man, and I'm just about done."

"What kind is it?"

"Pancreatic."

Jesus Christ. "So how can I help?"

"I want to end it."

"Euthanasia?"

Ray nodded.

Feeling conflicted now—knowing how terribly his friend must be suffering but not wanting to lose him, even to a solution he'd championed himself—Ben said, "I get it. I don't *like* it, but I get it." He sighed. "When were you thinking of doing it?"

Ray sighed now, too. "Month. Six weeks tops. Depends how bad it gets. I wanted some time to hang out with you guys—you especially—bullshit about old times and do juvenile shit like we did today. But if it gets much worse..."

"All right, look. Tomorrow, if you'd like, we'll head over to the Foundation. You can fill out the necessary forms, then I'll introduce you to Sandy Hart. Sandy's the best counselor we—"

Ray was shaking his head. "No counselors."

"No way around it. There are protocols—"

"Fuck protocols." He took Ben's hand in both of his; Ben could feel the disease smoldering in those once-powerful mitts and it broke his heart.

Then Ray dropped the bomb.

"I want you to do it," he said, his gaze steady, locked on Ben's widening eyes. "I want you to put me down."

FOUR

Thursday, June 1

ROXANNE WAS UP AND dressed the next morning before the sun cleared the horizon, making poached eggs
and toast for her and Gram. They ate in silence at the
breakfast nook Gramps had built when Roxanne was a
baby, each lost in her own musings on what was coming
and what had gone before.

They left their small yellow house on Second Avenue
at eight o'clock. Roxanne helped Gram into the passenger seat of the sporty red Honda Gramps had been so
fond of, then climbed in on the driver's side, securing
her seatbelt and helping Gram fasten hers. As she
backed onto the quiet street, it occurred to her that their
days in the house she loved so much were numbered,
Gram growing less able to maintain it on her own with
each passing month. In all likelihood, she'd be moving

the old gal into the Center before she left for Dalhousie in the fall.

The Center was a twenty-minute drive and Roxanne did it in twelve, an escalating urgency making her reckless and tense. By the time they pulled into the lot fronting the Euthanasia Foundation, her hands felt like they'd been stitched to the wheel.

She found a spot near the entrance and killed the engine. As she reached for the door handle, her grandmother said, "I can make it in from here on my own, sweetheart. Why don't you take off for a while and I'll call you when it's done."

Facing the old woman, Roxanne said, "Yesterday— even an hour ago—I might've said okay. But I want to see this through with you, Gram. You shouldn't have to go through it alone."

Gram gave her a stoic smile. "Honey, I mourned your grandfather ten months ago, when they told me he wouldn't be coming home." She glanced at the imposing building, its purpose undisguised by the cedar gardens and ornate exterior. Sighing, she said, "That isn't him in there anymore, my darling. It's just the place he used to live."

"I know that now. It just took me a little longer to figure out. I'm sorry I made you wait—"

"Please, Roxanne, don't *ever* apologize for that. You needed the time and I was happy to give it to you."

Roxanne nodded, the urge to cry welling up, then slipping away. Sitting in silence with her grandmother, she realized she really *had* said her goodbyes, and now it was time to move on. In the hope of softening the mood this morning, she'd prepared a ten-minute video spliced together from home movies dating as far back as the sixties, a surprise for Gram the Foundation said they'd screen during the euthanasia process.

Now Roxanne said, "Shall we?"

Nodding, Gram got out of the car.

* * *

Ben awoke fully dressed on the La-Z-Boy, the TV on but muted, an attractive brunette silently extolling the virtues of a bagless canister vacuum. The girl held him in thrall for a while, glistening lips shaping scripted words but somehow inviting intimacy, her obviously store-bought boobs shifting like fleshy zeppelins above her low-cut blouse, animated by her gesturing arms. It made him think of a book he'd read in the seventies called *Subliminal Seduction*, an exploration of the uses of sex in advertising, and he laughed out loud.

He grabbed the remote and switched the thing off, thinking, *They should write a new book and call it* Overt Seduction *or* Buy This Vacuum And I'll Bang You.

He leaned forward to bring the footrest down, the movement raising protests from his hip joints. His head spun for a moment once he was upright, and he braced himself against the armrest until the feeling passed. The next message his body sent came from his bladder, this one urgent, and he shuffled across the squeaky laminate flooring to the bathroom. He got his pants down as quickly as he could and lowered himself onto the cold plastic seat. Along with the numerous other indignities of aging, sitting down to pee seemed among the most humiliating, the loss of that great privilege of manhood—standing up to pee—diminishing him at some primal level. Maybe Ray was right. Maybe he *would*'ve made a nice little girl.

And it was there, sitting on the can with hot urine dribbling into the bowl, that he remembered the hash-addled promise he'd made to his dearest friend the night before.

"Okay, my brother. Okay. I'm not sure how yet, but I'll make it happen. Count on it."

Now he said, "Goddamn," and wadded a length of toilet paper into his fist, using it to dab himself dry, a singsong verse from childhood joining the rising cacophony in his head: *No matter how much you wiggle and jiggle and dance, the last three drops always land in your pants.*

He stood now, pulling up his drawers as he rose, quietly cursing the tiny squirt of urine spreading warm against his thigh.

What in the name of God had he let himself in for? There was no *way* he could legally euthanize his friend. He'd let his medical license expire a decade ago, and he knew without asking that Hicks would laugh him out of his office if he approached the man with the idea.

Ben made his way into the kitchen now and sat at the table, resting his head in his hands, replaying the details of the night before in his foggy mind. He'd explained the many drawbacks to Ray, telling him it was impossible, the best he could do was join him in the euthanasia theater. The whole thing was automated anyway, the technician sequestered in a booth remote from the theater itself, the drugs delivered via computerized pump. All he could do was ask the tech to leave the booth once he'd initiated the sequence. That way, at the end, they'd be totally alone.

But Ray had been adamant. "I want you to do it, Ben. Please. I don't want anyone else involved. Can you understand that? Just you and me, like old times. Just you and me."

Jesus Christ.

And he'd agreed?

Goddammit, yes, he'd agreed.

* * *

Later that morning, Ben scrambled off the La-Z-Boy to answer the phone, muting a blaring *Pawn Stars* episode with the remote.

It was Roxanne.

She said, "Still up for that lunch date?"

"Uh, yeah, you bet."

"Okay, good. I'm in the lobby. How long do you need?"

Ben glanced in the entryway mirror. He looked like hell, still in yesterday's clothes, thin hair a rat's nest, two days of stubble on his face.

He said, "Can you give me half an hour?"

"Take all the time you need, I've got my reader."

He said, "Okay," and almost signed off. Then: "Want to wait up here? It's quieter and I won't feel so rushed."

"Sure. Apartment ninety-twelve, right?"

"That's right. I'll leave the door unlocked. Just come ahead in."

She said, "I'll be right up," and Ben clutched his forehead, saying, "Oh my God, Roxanne, I can't believe I forgot. It was this morning, right? Your grandfather?" He heard her say, "Yes," in a small voice and said, "How did it go?"

Sounding steadier now, she said, "It went well, actually. In a strange way, it was almost like a formality. But now that it's over, Ben—if it's okay with you—I'd rather not talk about it anymore. At least not for now."

Ben said, "I can respect that. I just wanted to say I'm proud of you, Roxanne. And if you'd rather get together some other time..."

With a cheerfulness Ben could tell was at least partially manufactured, she said, "You're not squirming out of our date *that* easily, Doctor Hunter. Get yourself together and let's go see what's on the menu in the caf."

Ben said, "Ten-four, Roxie. Come ahead up."

Excited in spite of the circumstances, which instantly fled his mind, Ben cradled the receiver and unlocked the apartment door. Then he hustled into the bathroom for a shower.

* * *

When Ben emerged in his grey suit a half-hour later, Roxanne was sitting lotus-style in the La-Z-Boy, scanning something on her reader.

Feeling his face redden, Ben said, "You know, I had some fiction published in the eighties. Medical thrillers."

Roxanne beamed. "Really? Did you write under your own name?"

"Of course. Why give someone else the credit?"

Poking away at the reader now, Roxanne said, "*The Surgeon, Critical Care* and *Code Blue.* Any others?"

"That's the lot. But you don't want to read any of that stuff. So many bad words."

"Too late," Roxanne said, closing the reader and giving it a pat. "Got all three. And don't worry, I can handle a little foul language." She hopped off the chair, regarding him appraisingly now. "My, don't you look dapper."

"That's me," Ben said. "Dapper Sugar Willy."

Roxanne laughed and took his arm. "Shall we?"

Ben said, "We most certainly shall," and led her out of the apartment.

* * *

Though he was long retired, Ben still possessed a physician's mind—questing, analytical, viewing certain aspects of the human condition in terms of symptoms and diagnoses—and it occurred to him now, over a hot beef sandwich in the cafeteria, that he'd have to add Roxanne to his list of triggers, the time he'd spent with her so far almost consistently leading to one of those be-fuddling dislocations.

He could feel himself slipping now—watching her work unselfconsciously on a cob of corn, melted butter glazing her chin—drifting back to another time and an-other girl, one so much like Roxanne it made his head hurt.

Early in his geriatric practice, he'd come up with an analogy to help similarly afflicted patients better under-stand the mechanics of these 'spells'. He'd tell them that in the blank, suspended instant before they lost touch with reality, they were like a computer in reboot mode, but a reboot gone terribly awry. And when the brain returned to function, it was in a scrambled operating system, the reverse holding true when they came back from whatever archive of memory or madness they'd been banished to—if they came back at all. And it oc-curred to him now, as the same process claimed him, that it was a more apt analogy than he'd imagined. The only good thing about this particular attack was that Roxanne appeared not to notice, at least not as far as he could tell.

But then he was all the way gone and he said, "There's someone I want you to meet."

* * *

Startled by Ben's abrupt lunge to his feet, Roxanne said, "Can we finish our lunch first?"

"No time," Ben said, draping a napkin over her half-eaten meal. "This'll keep." He grabbed her hand. "Come on."

Hustling toward the elevators now, his grip on her hand almost painful, Roxanne felt like she was with a different person. A slightly crazy person. She could see it in his eyes as they boarded the elevator, a manic light intensified by the stark fluorescents. It was as if something was winding him up from the inside, compelling him along some frantic path. Cindy Gore, her best friend growing up, had gotten into cocaine their senior year, and Ben's behavior now reminded her of that. Between classes or at parties, Cindy would go into the bathroom her normal self and come out a few minutes later manic as hell. She was certain Ben wasn't snorting cocaine, but whatever was going on with him now, it was strange and a little scary.

A more likely explanation arose as he tugged her along the busy corridor, bumping shoulders with people without excusing himself. She'd noticed a bunch of pill bottles on the counter next to the kitchen sink while she was waiting for him to get ready. Maybe his behavior was being triggered by one of his meds or a combination of them, some bizarre interaction he wasn't aware of. Or maybe he was having a mini-stroke. Although his speech wasn't slurred, just really fast.

Genuinely worried now, she said, "Ben, what's going on?"

But he ignored her, punching the button for the fiftieth floor, saying, "She's in the penthouse. Says the light's better up there. She had to fight admin tooth and nail to get the place, too. Oh, my. You don't want to mess with Ely, she'll kick your ass. That's her name. Ely. She's an amazing artist, you're going to love her." Beaming like an adolescent, he said, "And she's going to love you—*oh*, I bet if I asked her, she'd do a portrait of you. In charcoal, maybe, or sepia. I love watching her work. It's like magic. I might even be able to talk her into doing you in oil."

She tried to reach him again on the elevator, saying, "Ben, can we slow down a minute and—"

But now the arrival chime sounded and the high-speed car eased to a stop. Roxanne's ears popped as the doors slid open and Ben's friends Quinn and Wilder stepped aboard, Quinn saying, "I *told* you the damn thing was going up," before noticing her and Ben. Grinning, Quinn said good morning, but Ben didn't respond, didn't even look at the guy.

The two old men glanced at Roxanne with obvious sorrow in their eyes, and she thought, *They know something*.

In a silence that was palpable now, Ben raised his eyes to the digital readout and the elevator resumed its ascent. The new arrivals stared at their shoes until the chime sounded again and Ben tugged Roxanne out on the fiftieth floor.

As if nothing strange had happened, he said, "She's right down here, fifty-oh-two," and led her to the artist's door. He raised his fist to knock, then glanced at Roxanne, that manic gleam still in his eyes. Whispering

94

now, he said, "I should warn you, though. The woman curses like a dock worker."

* * *

Quinn said, "Jesus," as the elevator doors slid shut. "I've never seen him that bad." He poked the lighted button for the cafeteria level.

Wilder nodded. "Son of a bitch had no idea who we were."

"And the other day? On the way to the greenhouse? I had to shout in the man's face to bring him back. There one minute, gone the next. I'm sure he thinks we don't know. And I'm worried he's going to hurt that sweet kid."

"How so?"

Quinn shook his head. "You know, for such a smartass, you can be dumb as a stump sometimes."

"You think I won't slap those dentures out of your pie hole?"

"Relax, man. You don't see what's going on with those two?"

"Clearly not."

"The girl doesn't put you in mind of anyone?" Wilder gave him an exasperated look and Quinn said, "Think Hillcrest High and broken-hearted Ben. The Sadie Hawkins dance? Where it all started. November sixty-seven. Or maybe it was sixty-eight. Christ, I'm halfway demented myself."

"No argument there."

Quinn said, "Blow me," and waited, letting it sink into the man's thick skull. It wasn't until the elevator came
to a stop and the opening doors admitted the clatter of
the cafeteria that Quinn saw enlightenment dawn in his
friend's dark eyes.

"Oh, shit," Wilder said. "You might be right."

"Of course I'm right. It's as plain as the nose on your
face."

Silent now, the men shuffled out and the doors ran
shut behind them. Wilder made a beeline for the coffee
machine and Quinn headed for the fresh-fruit display.
They reconvened in the check-out lane, not speaking
again until they were seated at their usual table by the
windows.

Spooning out a scoop of melon, Quinn said, "Are you
going to tell him?"

"Fuck, no."

"Yeah, me neither."

Now Wilder said, "Why not get *him* to do it?" and
thrust his chin toward the check-out lane. Quinn turned
to see Ray Gale with a food tray in his hands, scanning
the sunlit room for a familiar face.

Grinning, Quinn said, "What I said earlier? I take it
back. You're a goddamn genius." He got to his feet and
waved Ray over.

* * *

Ely was struggling to capture a speck of sunlight on
the eagle's yellow beak, her trembling hand refusing to

cooperate on this fine detail. She blamed the slew of medications they had her on, those pushy pharmacy techs banging on her door three times a day, making her gobble handfuls of capsules and pills, some of them big enough to choke a horse. Typical of the staff here, they all thought she was feeble, just a crusty old bull-dyke lesbian playing paint-by-the-numbers all day.

But Ely was no feeb. Not *this* old New Yorker. She'd learned to use a computer before most of these snot-noses were born, and she'd Googled some of the poi-sons they had her on. And she was convinced that one of them—a green-and-white capsule that tasted like ass—was responsible for her tremor. An anti-psychotic, of all things. For senility, the doctor told her. "After all, Ely, you *are* a hundred-and-two." Condescending wea-sel. When she complained about the tremor a few weeks later, the man told her she'd just have to live with it.

Live with this, Ely thought now, raising her middle finger, stretching it out as straight as it would go, which wasn't very straight anymore.

She rested her brush on the easel and sat back in her motorized chair, tilting her neck from side to side to work out a kink.

'Intention tremor', they called it. She'd looked that up, too. Could recite its meaning by rote, which she did now at the top of her lungs. "The amplitude of an inten-tion tremor increases as an extremity approaches the endpoint of a visually guided movement. You dipshits." It meant your damn hand shook when you tried to do something delicate. She'd even figured out a way to assess the severity of the condition in herself.

Ely reached for a speck of lint on the arm of the black hoodie she'd painted in for the past thirty years, a fine-motor skill she'd been practicing since she started tonguing the capsules into the corner of her mouth and spitting them into the toilet after the techs were gone. Two weeks now. The tremor began when her fingers were about an inch-and-a-half from the lint, the movement barely perceptible at first, then coarsening as she closed the distance.

Taking her time, Ely touched the fabric, pinched—and *got* the little sucker this time, thinking, *Thank God, it's going away.* She chortled. *Should be good as new in a week.*

There was a knock at the door now and Ely glanced at the clock on the mantle: the drug pushers weren't due for another hour. She thought, *Must be Ben,* and hollered, "It's open," in her big, bawdy voice.

* * *

Several things went through Ely's mind as Ben came through the door, dressed to the nines with a young girl in tow, but principle among them was a sense that something was terribly wrong. She knew he'd been having increasingly troublesome skirmishes with Alzheimer's—she'd been his trusted confidant since he was a teenager, and had witnessed a few episodes herself—

but the bout he was having now was clearly among the worst of them.

Tugging the girl along by the hand, he tramped into the room saying, "Ely, I'd like you to meet my new friend, uh…" He turned a quizzical eye on the girl and she said, "Hi, Ely, I'm Roxanne Austen. Ben and I met at the anniversary celebration the other day."

The girl offered her hand and Ely shook it, saying, "Nice to meet you, honey." She glanced at Ben. "Now what lies has this old fart told you about me?"

Ben laughed too loud and too long and Ely said, "Sit your ass in that chair, Hunter, you're making me nervous. And let go of the girl's hand, you're cutting off the circulation."

Chastened, Ben released Roxanne's hand and plunked onto the chair. Noticing the painting Ely was working on, he said, "Oh, wow, Ely, that's fantastic. What is that, a flamingo?"

Ely waited to see if he was trying to be funny, then said, "Flamingos are pink, and they don't land in trees." She said to Roxanne, "Sweetheart, there's a pot of tea on the stove. Be a lamb and go heat it up for us, would you? Cups are on the shelf over the sink."

Roxanne said, "Sure," and scooted around the room divider into the kitchen.

Now Ely said, "Hunter, come here," and Ben did, moving over to stand beside her. Ely caught him by the wrist. She said, "Closer, down here," and when he stooped, she slapped him across the face.

Ben said, *"Uh,"* and his eyes cleared. Rubbing his cheek, he regarded her with frank perplexity, as if seeing her for the first time. He said, "Was I...?"

Ely nodded. "Bad this time."

Ben glanced toward the kitchen, a clink of cutlery out there now. Ely said, "You brought your new friend," and he gave her that puzzled look again. She said, "Roxanne," and he nodded, the last of the cobwebs falling away. "You need to do something about this, Ben."

"I know. But there's nothing I *can* do." He glanced at the painting. "My God, Ely, you haven't lost your touch. That is so beautiful. Did you know bald eagles can live up to twenty years in the wild?"

"Sit," Ely said, Roxanne on her way back now, spoons chattering against china. "We'll talk about this later."

PART TWO

FIVE

AS IT TURNED OUT, Ben didn't discuss his condition with Ely again until weeks later, deep into the month of June. The spells continued to plague him, increasing in frequency and duration during that unseasonably hot stretch. But between hanging out with Ray, and spending whatever time he could with Roxanne, he barely had a moment alone with Ely. And truth be told, he had little interest in broaching the subject with her again. Ever. Because in spite of the fact that he could only remember fragments of the episodes once they'd passed, the bits he *could* recall were consistently more exhilarating than the time he spent in the 'real' world. When you got right down to it, what was so wrong with feeling young again? With reliving past triumphs and joys? Besides, Ely was like a dog with a bone. If he didn't give her time to fixate on something else—her meds were always a safe bet—she'd hound him to the grave.

So he elected to keep his distance for a while, let the dust settle. Though he still wanted her to paint Roxanne. The girl was the first person he'd cared about in a long time, and he wanted to give her something special, something she could look at after he was gone and perhaps think fondly of him. She was like the daughter he never had, and he treasured every moment he spent with her.

He'd give it a few weeks, then approach Ely again. Soften her up with a box of those Häagen-Dazs treats she loved so much.

* * *

With the exception of Roxanne coming into his life, Ray moving into the Center was the best thing that had happened to Ben in over a decade. His abrupt transition from fulltime practice into retirement had derailed him, and in spite of his best efforts, he'd never fully gotten back on track. His life as a physician had fulfilled him, not only professionally but socially as well. Since he'd never married, he'd come to think of his fellow staff members as family; it was the principal reason he'd moved into the Center instead of retiring to the winterized cottage he owned west of Ottawa, a property he'd hung onto after selling the townhouse he'd called home for thirty-eight years. And at first it had been good, meeting colleagues for lunch in the cafeteria or joining them for outings and parties. But most of that gang was gone now, either dead or retired. And the new crew, while they knew who he was and respected him for it, often made him feel like he was getting in the way. So eventually, he just stayed away.

Having his high school buddies onsite was a plus—and sometimes a hoot, like the other day outside the greenhouse—but in small doses only. Those guys could be exhaustingly juvenile. Even growing up, it had always been Ray he was closest to.

But for the first few days following Ray's impassioned plea for euthanasia, Ben had deliberately avoided the man. Partly because he needed time to process the gravity of his friend's request; but also because Ray had confronted him out of the blue with the perverse notion that he was using Roxanne as some kind of substitute for a girl he'd dated in high school, and it ticked him off. It was clear Quinn and Wilder had put him up to it, both of them lurking in the background while Ray raised their ridiculous assertion. This was on the day after he introduced Roxanne to Ely, the three of them showing up on his doorstep like reluctant executioners, the two cowards skulking off to raid the fridge while Ray passed judgment in the living room.

Sure, he'd had one of his spells that day; he was aware of the missing time. And it was clear the guys knew what was going on with him now, though he'd only ever discussed it with Ray. Which meant his best friend had not only betrayed a confidence, he'd allowed himself to be swayed by those grinning yard apes. Quinn and Wilder had been in the apartment when Ben went into anaphylactic shock from the medication, and it was Wilder's quick thinking that saved his life. But he'd never actually *talked* to them about the disease. It was just one of those things you didn't discuss, like alcoholism or AIDS, particularly in a community like the Geriatric Center, where the specter of Alzheimer's hung over every head in the place. Because to those not already afflicted, it seemed that to even utter the name of the beast—especially in the presence of someone in the early stages themselves—was to somehow invite it into their own lives. Like a contagion or maybe a vampire. And even with the proven success of the current treatment regimens, the prospect of slipping into the remote alternate universe that was dementia was a source of low-grade terror for everyone.

But none of that justified his friends' cruel accusation, and he'd promptly tossed them out on their asses, saying if they ever brought it up again, they'd be dead to him. Every last one of them.

* * *

So he fumed for a couple of days, pouted for a couple more, then took unwitting advantage of the primary symptom of dementia—memory loss—and picked up the pieces with his buddies as if nothing had happened.

Through the balance of June, he and Ray fell into a casual routine, first convening in the cafeteria for breakfast—Ben having a bagel and tea, Ray loading up on bacon and eggs, home fries and white toast lathered in butter. "Who gives a shit, Benji? It's not like I need to watch my cholesterol anymore."—then trekking out to the falls to reminisce. There was always a lot of laughter. Ray was incredibly funny, his round face as pliable as Silly Putty. And he loved to fool around.

On occasion, though, their discussions turned serious. One hot day toward the middle of June, Ray brought up the thing with Roxanne again, saying it was pretty obvious Ben got confused around her sometimes. In his defense, Ben said he got confused around *everyone* lately, he had Alzheimer's disease for Christ's sake. But Ray persisted, risking Ben's fury again—and it was there, just below the surface.

"I know you see it," Ray said. "It's in the girl's eyes. And that smile. The first time I laid eyes on her, I thought of Melanie Anderson."

"Melanie was sixty years ago, Ray. I'm over it."

"Are you?"

"*Yes*. Now would you drop it, please?"

"Because I don't think you *are* over it. Maybe when you're yourself you are. But this girl...she triggers you somehow. Not always. But when she does, it's like watching you when you were a teenager. It's freaky."

"*Please.*"

"All right. But you're going to break the kid's heart, and I know you don't wanna do that."

"I'm about to break your arm."

"*Okay*. Bitch."

"Dipshit."

Ray lapsed into silence for a minute, then said, "You know what I think?"

"That I'm a sentimental old fool?"

"No. I think when we get older, there's a natural desire to go back. Or maybe it runs deeper than that. Maybe it's hardwired into our genes. I think our purest selves are children, filled with love and wonder, the way we start out. And I think that child remains inside each of us as we age. In a sense, we become its caretaker. Neglectful ones, usually. Because we get busy with *serious* things. School, romantic love, making ends meet. And the years fly by. And pretty soon we lose touch with that child. We can't see through its eyes anymore. So it goes to sleep. Hibernates, maybe. But it's still there, waiting. Waiting for all that shit to fall away.

"And one day, decades down the road, we find ourselves alone—even if we're surrounded by people who love us—staring our mortality in the face. But if we're lucky, *really* lucky, we rediscover that forgotten child, sleeping in the dark. It's why you see such horrible things on Florida beaches. Old bastards sucking back margaritas and strutting around with their droopy asses hanging out. Because they've found that child and embraced it, and now they just don't *care*."

Ben said, "Adolescence revisited."

"Well...yeah."

"Honestly, Ray, that's a beautiful notion. I mean it. And I think if anybody's managed to keep their inner child thriving, it's you. But what has any of that got to do with me and Roxanne?"

"Nothing, really. I just felt like waxing poetic."

"You really are a dipshit, you know it?"

108

Ray grinned. "Naw, I'm just a kid." He rested a hand on Ben's wrist. "But listen, Benji, I get it. If I could go back, I would. I mean, who *would*n't? But I can't. And neither can you, outside of your mind. Or your disease. And using Roxanne to get there can only end badly for you both."

* * *

Most mornings between about nine and ten, Quinn and Wilder would catch up with Ray and Ben and they'd all head over to the rec center for a few games of snooker, then move on to the food court to girl-watch and lie about past conquests.

For Ben, the truly heartbreaking part of those days was witnessing Ray's precipitous decline: the weight loss accelerating at a staggering rate; those merry eyes retreating like hunted rodents into their bony sockets; the antic energy the man had always possessed fizzling like a doused coal. At three in the morning on June twenty-first, Ray appeared at Ben's door in his pajama bottoms and said he couldn't hack it much longer, then drifted down the hallway like an apparition. What made it worse for Ben was that he frequently forgot the severity of his friend's condition, and was repeatedly forced to confront it anew.

In the midst of all this, it was Roxanne who gave him the will to carry on. Most days, depending on which shift she was working, he'd meet her for lunch, turning the hour they gave her into an event, sometimes bringing picnic food he'd prepared the night before, sometimes sitting with her in the cafeteria munching burgers and fries. Roxanne liked to talk, and Ben was happy to listen. She told him about her grandfather and how much he, Ben, reminded her of the man. She described at length the courses she'd be taking in the fall, and showed him pictures of the Dalhousie campus she'd downloaded onto her phone.

At the end of her day shift on the twenty-second, Roxanne ran up to him red-faced in the lobby with a folded sheet of white bond in her hand, telling him she'd been awarded a full scholarship by the university. Ben scanned the letter with a grin on his face. When he handed the letter back, Roxanne hugged him and said they should celebrate. Ben agreed, suggesting they cab into the city that very night, go to Al's Steakhouse on Elgin Street and chow down in style. Roxanne asked if she could bring her grandmother along and Ben said of course, he'd love to meet the woman and tell her what a great job she'd done raising her granddaughter.

Tucking the letter into her knapsack, Roxanne said, "No need to pay for a cab. We can take Gram's car. What time works for you?"

"I'll make the reservation for seven."

"Then it's a date. I'll pick you up at six-thirty."

And she was gone.

Ben was still smiling when he got back to the apartment and glanced at the clock on the microwave.

Five-thirteen. Time to get ready.

As he got undressed, he wondered what Roxanne's grandmother would be like. Then he padded into the bathroom, singing an old Beatles tune under his breath.

"She loves you, yeah, yeah, yeah ..."

When he stepped out of the shower ten minutes later, he was startled by his own reflection in the steam-fogged mirror. In the soothing hiss and splash of the shower, he'd been wandering the back avenues of his memory...cycling actually, climbing a steep hill in Vermont behind his girl, watching her work the pedals with those long legs, remembering their warm strength as they encircled his waist in the tent the night before, the tiny moans she uttered as he moved inside her...

Oh, God.

He slipped a towel off the rack and used it to clear a porthole in the steamy mirror—and in that first instant, a total stranger returned his stare, the effect so alarming, Ben believed he was standing naked in front of a window and some dirty old man had been watching him shower.

Then it dawned, as it had so often in the recent past, only to duck below the horizon again to catch him unawares.

That's me.

With a kind of defiant vigor, he toweled off a wider area of the mirror, polishing the surface to a telling gleam, revealing the old man he'd become: stooped; wrinkled; liver-spotted; grey.

Staring into those faded eyes, he became aware of a furious debate going on inside his head—yearning versus despondency—each side tugging at him now, seeking to tip him off the knife-edge of his sanity. It troubled him deeply, making him fearful of losing his grip for good. Making him believe his friends had been right.

Then, quite audibly, a door slammed shut in his mind, silencing the quarrelsome voices. And now another voice, this one barely above a whisper.

Fuck it.

He wrapped the towel around his waist, grabbed the toothpaste and deodorant and switched off the bathroom light. From now on he'd brush his teeth in the kitchen. There were no mirrors in there. No tired old men leering back at him.

He had a date with a beautiful girl, and no 'concerned' friend or nattering inner voice was going to take that away from him.

Not now. Not ever.

* * *

Ben was sweating in his suit jacket when the phone rang at precisely 6:30. Roxanne was waiting for him in the lobby, standing with her back to him by the floor-to-ceiling windows, haloed in evening light. She was wearing a coral-red dress, cashmere with a zipper down the back, the hem suspended an inch above her knees. She had her hair down tonight, a tapered cascade that almost reached her hips.

When she turned to face him, Ben felt his insides plummet, the sensation bringing to mind a long-ago summer he'd spent as a dunk-tank clown, the visceral thrill that drenched him now no less bracing than the icy water in that tank. She carried a tiny sequined clutch, letting it rest against her thigh, and when she took his arm he caught a whiff of jasmine.

Smiling, Roxanne said, "Gram couldn't make it tonight. She's not feeling well."

Good. "Nothing serious, I hope."

"Migraine. I offered to stay home with her, but she insisted we go ahead."

Good again. "Next time," Ben said, holding the door open for her.

"Next time for sure."

* * *

Ben had been a loyal patron of Al's Steakhouse since it opened in 1967. In that time, he'd seen the place undergo numerous facelifts and personnel changes. But the fundamental constant was the beef, always the beef. The finest on the planet. Opening the door for Roxanne, he felt like one of Pavlov's dogs, the smoky aroma of chargrilled steak flooding his mouth with saliva.

He'd requested his usual spot, an intimate booth at the back of the restaurant, away from the bustle and clatter of the main dining area. As Roxanne slid into the plush leather seat across from him, Ben pointed out the rogues' gallery on the adjacent wall, dozens of framed photographs of the proprietor with some of the famous faces that had dined here.

Pointing at one of the photos, Ben said, "You know who this guy is?"

Roxanne shook her head. "That's quite the hairdo, though."

"That's Gene Simmons, bass player for the rock band Kiss." Roxanne shrugged and Ben shook his head, saying, "Oh my, the youth of today."

Laughing, Roxanne pointed at another photo. "Okay, smarty-pants, who's this right here?"

Ben squinted at a color shot of a heavily made-up woman with what appeared to be a braided mop on her head and iridescent fish scales for eyebrows. He said, "Bride of Frankenstein?" and Roxanne laughed so explosively she sprayed him with spit.

Leaning across the table to dab his face with a napkin, she said, "That's Lady Gaga."

"Lady what?"

"*Ga*ga. She's young in this shot. She must be forty now, but she's still going strong."

"What does she do? Model Halloween costumes?"

"She's a *sing*er. Very famous. I can't believe you never heard of—"

"Good evening, folks. My name is Russ and I'll be your server tonight."

Ben shot the waiter a dirty look—nothing like interrupting a person in the middle of a sentence—but the kid's eyes were glued to Roxanne. Ben knew the type: bright, good-looking, cocky as hell.

The kid was holding a pitcher of ice water, and now he leaned in to fill their glasses, starting with Roxanne's.

That done, he set the pitcher on the table and struck a quizzical pose, saying, "Roxanne, right? Roxanne Austen? Greely Elementary?"

Ben watched her cheeks flush red, perplexity pinching her features, and he almost told the kid to send over a different waiter.

But Roxanne was smiling now, saying, "Russell *Ames*? My *God*. Eighth grade, right? Mrs. Skrim's homeroom class?"

"Right," Russ said, returning Roxanne's smile. "If memory serves, you were pretty much the teacher's pet in that class."

Roxanne's blush deepened. "I *was* a bit of a brown-noser."

"I wouldn't've put it that way. Smartest kid in the school, maybe, but never a brown-noser."

Roxanne laughed, that big, unselfconscious laugh Ben loved. She said, "No, I was a brown-noser," and now Russ laughed too.

Glancing at *him* now, Russ said, "Is this your grandfather?" and Ben wanted to knock the perfect white teeth out of the brat's GQ coverboy face.

Roxanne said, "No," and apologized to Ben, saying she hadn't meant to ignore him. "This is my friend, Ben Hunter. He's a doctor."

The kid offered a handshake and Ben accepted it, the little showoff almost crushing his fingers.

Still pumping Ben's hand, Russ said, "A doctor, eh?" and looked again at Roxanne. "Well, you may come in handy tonight, sir, because there's a good chance I'll be getting my heart broken."

Ben thought, *Jesus, does ham-fisted shit like that actually work?* But Roxanne was blushing like a schoolgirl.

Tugging his hand away, Ben said, "We'd like to see menus, please."

Russ said, "Of course," and handed over the menus tucked under his arm. "Would you like to hear the specials?"

Roxanne started to say something and Ben said, "Maybe later," getting some edge in his tone.

Russ picked up on the vibe, saying, "Take all the time you need." And with a nod at Roxanne, he moved away.

She seemed uncomfortable now, and Ben felt guilty for being so abrupt. He said, "I'm sorry, Roxanne. I realize you know the kid, but the way he interrupted you, that was just rude."

Turning to watch Russ move toward the bar, Roxanne said, "That's okay. I barely remember the guy. He was a pimple-faced clown in eighth grade, that much I *do* remember." She sipped some water through a straw, then glanced the kid's way again, saying, "He certainly has changed."

Ben wished they'd gone to McDonald's.

Roxanne turned her attention to the menu now, saying, "What do you recommend?"

"Steak," Ben said, trying to let it go. "Any kind you like. The bacon-wrapped filet melts in your mouth."

"Then I'll have the filet." She closed the menu and slid it to the edge of the table.

Ben followed suit, saying, "It's settled, then. Filets all around."

He tried to salvage the mood after that, but Roxanne was quiet now, maybe even a little annoyed. He wanted to fix it somehow, get her laughing again, but he couldn't think of anything to say. She kept sipping her water, then glancing toward the bar, as if searching for that strutting peckerwood. She even checked her phone a couple of times, something Ben had always found rude and disrespectful, something she'd never done in his presence before.

Inevitably, the waiter showed up again, approaching the table from behind Ben this time, tricking him into thinking Roxanne's pleased smile was intended for him.

Verging on anger now, Ben made things worse by ordering for both of them, asking Roxanne how she wanted her steak done, not letting the kid do his job. When the kid left, Roxanne excused herself, saying she wanted to call home to see how Gram was doing.

Feeling like a fool, Ben watched to see where she went, afraid she was looking for the waiter. But she headed for the washroom, raising the phone to her ear as she moved out of sight. Ben tried to think of what he'd say when she got back, maybe ask how her grandmother was doing.

But the food arrived just as she did, one of the chefs bringing it out, a chubby guy with an Italian accent who seemed to know Ben. "Good to see you again, Doctor

Hunter," the chef said. "It's been too long." Ben tried to be polite, but he couldn't recall ever meeting the man. By the time the guy left, waddling penguin-like through the double kitchen doors, the tension in the booth seemed impenetrable.

Now Roxanne said, "Gram's fine. She took a nap and now her headache's gone."

Hating the quaver in his voice, Ben said, "That's good."

"She's such a sweetheart. I'd love the two of you to meet."

Realizing Roxanne was being the adult now, Ben said, "I look forward to it. Maybe we can work out a lunch date, just the three of us."

"That would be nice." Slicing her steak, Roxanne said, "Is everything okay, Ben?"

He thought, *Be careful*. "Of course. Why do you ask?"

"I don't know. You just seem…out of sorts."

He said, "To be honest, I think the pharmacy tech that works my floor has been replacing my B-twelve tablets with birth control pills."

Roxanne laughed and Ben felt a weight lift off his chest.

She said, "Oh, really? Feeling a tad bloated, are we?"

He nodded, running with it, adding a flagrantly gay lilt to his voice now. "That and my nipples. You know." He ran a hand across his chest. "So sensitive."

And for a while, they were okay again.

* * *

Roxanne said she was too full for dessert, but Ben had a bowl of butterscotch ice cream, his favorite since childhood. Russ showed up a couple more times, but his behavior was more professional now—though he did flash Roxanne a flirtatious smile when he brought the ice cream, making her blush again.

When the bill came, Roxanne offered to pick up the tab, saying she was flush now, the scholarship money allowing her to splurge a little. But Ben firmly objected, tucking his credit card into the discrete black folder the waiter had left. Then he excused himself, saying he had to visit the boys' room.

Trying to disguise his feebleness as he stood, he shuffled off to the bathroom, cursing his traitorous bladder. He'd put up with it as long as he could, but in the past few minutes that full sensation had ripened into frank discomfort, and it was either go to the can *right now* or wet his pants.

Russ was on his way out of the bathroom as Ben got to the door. The kid smiled and gave him a congenial nod, holding the door open for him. The little bastard smelled like a spring breeze.

* * *

Russ said, "I don't think your doctor friend likes me."

Roxanne could feel her face turning red again. She hated that about herself. She said, "I'm sure he likes you just fine. He's normally sweet as can be. He just seems, I don't know, not quite himself tonight."

She thought, *Understatement,* and watched the muscles flex in Russ's tan forearm as he picked up Ben's dessert dish. He caught her looking and her face grew even redder, sweat blooming on her forehead now in a prickly film.

This guy is so dreamy.

He tucked the bill folder under his arm and started away, *his* cheeks looking red now too, though it was hard to tell in the tastefully-muted ambient light.

Then he was facing her again, saying, "I realize this is sudden, Roxanne. I mean, we barely know each other and—God, I could lose my job for this, but—"

Touching his arm, Roxanne said, "I'd love to see you again, Russ," relieved to be the one holding the trump card now. "Can I borrow your pen?"

He plucked an *Al's Steakhouse* ballpoint out of his vest pocket and passed it to her with a shaky hand. Roxanne laughed, the excitement making her giddy. She scribbled her number on a paper napkin and handed it to him, watching as he first made certain he could read it, then tucked it into the hip pocket of the trim black dress pants he was wearing.

He thanked her now—and yes, he *was* blushing—saying he'd give her a call soon. When she tried to return the pen, he said, "Your friend'll be needing that for the bill."

* * *

Ben made a point of avoiding the mirror. He got his business done—sitting in a stall like a girl—sprinkled water on his fingers, and got the hell out of there.

Access to the bathrooms was tastefully concealed behind a series of stained-glass panels, and when Ben got to the end of them he saw the waiter at their booth again, handing something to Roxanne. It looked like a pen, and at first he thought she was being a sneak, trying to pay for the meal herself. Smiling, he started toward the booth to put a stop to it. The evening had been his idea, he should be the one footing the bill.

But now he saw her jot something on a napkin and he froze, watching as she handed it to the waiter, the kid giving it a quick look before tucking it away. He thought, *She's giving him her number*, and felt rage rise up in him like a taunted demon, and he wanted to lash out, make the kid pay for his audacity—

Then he glanced at his hands, curled into feeble fists, and felt something fracture inside him, his impotent fury suspended on one side, some unbearable truth shedding its cloak on the other. He looked away, trying to hang on to the *vitality* the rage had awakened in him.

But it was no use.

He looked again at his hands, the bony fingers uncurling now, the action impeded by arthritis.

Shaken, despondent, he returned to the booth, added a generous tip to the bill and asked Roxanne to drive him home. She tried to make conversation during the twenty-minute trek, and Ben did his best to play along.

But he was hurt and angry...and it wasn't long before he had no idea why.

Roxanne pulled up in front of his apartment building and thanked him for a lovely evening. She asked if he wanted her to walk him inside and he told her he wasn't a little girl. He struggled with his seatbelt for a weighted moment, then got it undone and heaved himself out of the car, shrugging off Roxanne's helping hand.

The metallic thud of the closing door was the loneliest sound he'd ever heard.

* * *

Roxanne navigated the drive home through a veil of tears. Hurt and confused, she kept replaying the evening in her mind and arriving at the same bewildering conclusion: *He's jealous.*

But it didn't make sense. Ben was four times her age, and—most of the time—the parameters of their relationship were both natural and clear. He was like a father to her, and she loved him for it. He'd come into her life at exactly the right moment, and, perhaps *because* he was so much like Gramps, had slipped willingly, even gratefully, into the role. In that regard, they were a perfect fit.

But sometimes...well, things got weird. Like the day he brought her up to meet Ely. Or that afternoon by the falls when he asked her to go steady, then wrote it off to daydreaming.

Or tonight. Especially tonight. For a while there, she'd felt like she was out with a jealous boyfriend. It was ludicrous and deeply twisted...

But there it was.

No. You're being paranoid. Ben's not like that. Not at all.

It was true. She *was* being paranoid. Ben was no more a dirty old man than she was a brain surgeon. He was always the perfect gentleman.

It had to be something else.

Pulling into the driveway at home, a light drizzle falling now, Roxanne wondered again if he might be having mini-strokes, like the ones Gramps had suffered before the big one took him down for good. TIAs, the doctors called them. Transient Ischemic Attacks. It seemed a perfectly reasonable explanation. The mini-strokes had presented differently in her grandfather—numbness on one side of his face, temporary loss of vision—but she'd looked it up on the Internet and knew TIAs could also present as confusion or flash personality changes.

Worried now, she wondered if she should head back to the Center, insist he go to the emergency room.

Yes, do it.

It occurred to her then to call him first, see if she could get a sense of how he was doing. Maybe he was just having a bad day and she was fretting over nothing.

Concern flared again when by the seventh ring he hadn't picked up, and she pictured him sprawled facedown on the kitchen floor, his brain slowly dying like her grandfather's had—

But then he answered and she said, "Ben?" a little too stridently.

"Roxanne! It's so *nice* to hear from you."

She was mute for a long moment, her thought processes stalled by the sheer unexpectedness of what she was hearing. The man on the phone sounded exactly nothing like the one she'd dropped off at the Center less than a half hour before.

"Roxanne? Still there?"

"Yes, Ben, sorry. I guess I was..."

"Daydreaming?" He laughed. "Don't I know what *that's* like. To what do I owe the honor?"

"I, uh...I was just wondering how you were doing."

"Well, aren't you a doll. I was just thinking about how we should celebrate your scholarship. There's this wonderful restaurant downtown: Al's Steakhouse. Ever heard of it?"

SIX

Thursday, June 29

BEN SAID, "ELY, I'VE got a huge favor to ask."

Ely glared at him over her horn rims. The eagle painting was almost done—she was adding pine needles to the bird's perch now, a repetitive task requiring her full attention—and the man was driving her crazy. She said, "Hunter, how many times do I have to tell you not to *hover* when I'm trying to work?"

Curled on the couch with her reader, Roxanne stifled a laugh.

Ben shuffled back a few steps and Ely said, "Thank you. Now what is it you want?"

He said, "How would you feel about doing a portrait of Roxanne?"

Roxanne flushed cherry-red.

Ben said, "I was thinking in oil."

Huffing, the artist plucked the glasses off her nose, letting the neck strap take their weight. Now she turned to squint at Roxanne, as if measuring her. "And how does the young lady feel about all this?"

Roxanne stammered, clearly caught off guard, and Ely could tell Ben hadn't discussed it with her yet, not at any length. He'd pulled this same sort of stunt in the seventies, after losing the girl he'd hoped to marry. He'd gone off the deep end for a while, drinking too much, smoking pot, and leading an endless parade of 'girl-friends' up to her Gatineau Hills lake house, trying to impress them with his edgy lesbian artist friend. He'd pester her to sketch them, nude if they'd allow it—that part she'd never complained about—then try to get into their pants in the spare bedroom in the loft. It had been as if he were trying to fuck away the heartache.

As this recollection played out in Ely's mind, she believed she understood what was going on between Ben and Roxanne—and she knew exactly how she was going to handle it. She loved the man like a son, always had, but he needed an awakening. And she was just the person to give it to him. He'd thank her in the end.

A week ago, he'd come to her like a scared kid, telling her how Roxanne had turned up on his doorstep the night before, insisting he go to the emergency room. How she then tried to convince him they'd been out to dinner earlier that same evening, and finally forced him to check his wallet, where she'd seen him tuck the credit card receipt. And how his last clear recollection of that day, before Roxanne showed up at his apartment, was of the girl running up to him in the lobby to tell him about her scholarship. "And I *still* can't remember having dinner with her," he said, a bewildered glaze in his eyes. "Any of it. I've had memory lapses before, Ely, and we both know why. But never like this. We're talking hours here. *Hours.*"

Ely had sensed there was more to it than that, and got the full story from Roxanne later that day. They sat together by the Koi pond during the kid's lunch break and Roxanne gave her all the grim details, culminating with Ben acting like a jilted boyfriend when he saw her flirting with the waiter.

"Russ is a really nice guy, Ely," Roxanne told her. "I'm going to be seeing him again, and I want Ben to like him too, you know?"

But Ely had darker things on her mind. Never one to skirt a delicate subject, she asked Roxanne if Ben had ever made a move on her.

"What do you mean?"

"Sexually. Has the old bastard ever tried to put his hands on you?"

"God, Ely, *no*. It's not like that."

"What is it like, then?"

Roxanne stared at her hands, as if searching them for answers. She said, "It's not all the time. Only when he has these episodes. The first couple of times, I thought it was just old age, you know? My grandmother gets a little weird sometimes, too. She calls it mental doddering. But when it happens to Ben, it's like...it's like I'm not even there. I mean, *he's* the one who's not there. The real

Ben." She regarded Ely with genuine concern. "When it happens, I get the feeling he's stuck somewhere in the past, and I just...provoke it somehow. Do you know what I mean?"

Ely said, "I believe I do."

"But, no, he's never even hugged me. Sometimes I hold his hand, and if we do hug, it's always me who initiates."

"Word of advice? No more touching. Of any kind."

Roxanne nodded, but Ely could see she didn't like it. She really did love the old boy. For all his many quirks, Ben Hunter was easy to love. Or maybe it was just an indicator of how much the girl missed her grandfather. Probably an equal measure of both.

It was clear Ben hadn't told the girl about his condition yet, and she was betting pride would prevent him from *ever* telling her. But Ely didn't feel it was her place to do so in his stead. At least not yet.

As if to confirm the assumption, Roxanne told her she'd finally convinced him to go to the ER that night, saying the doctor told him the spells were most likely the result of a drug interaction, and suggested he stop taking his anti-depressant medication for a few weeks to see if it made any difference.

Ely said, "Were you *in* the room when the doctor said all this?"

"No. Ben asked me to wait in the lounge." She smiled. "I don't think he wanted me to see him with his shirt off. Why do you ask?"

Ely said, "Just curious," and thought, *Hunter, you old liar. Get ready for a good swift kick in the balls.*

* * *

Roxanne was saying something now, and Ely tuned her in.

"I'd love you to paint me, Ely, but I'm sure you're already very busy. And I'm not—"

Ely raised a hand, cutting the girl off, a plan of action taking shape in her mind. "Actually, sweetie, I'd *love* to paint you. You're a classic beauty. And the light worships you." She glanced at Ben, the man grinning like a dummy now, and said, "You know what? Why don't I paint the *two* of you, together," stifling a laugh when the girl's face lit up and Hunter's almost slid off his skull.

They were all talking at the same time now, Roxanne saying, "Oh, Ely, that would be so *great*," Ben saying, "No, *I* don't want to be in it," Ely taking the girl's side, saying, "Come on, Hunter, don't be a spoilsport."

They bickered back and forth for a while, until Ely said, "All *right*. If the big baby doesn't wanna be in the painting, the big baby doesn't have to *be* in the painting. God, Hunter, you're such an old woman."

Roxanne took one last shot, glancing doe-eyed at Ben with her bottom lip stuck out, and Ben said, "Tuck in that lip, young lady, or a bird's gonna come along and land on it. Maybe an eagle."

Now Ely said to Roxanne, "Okay, honey, forget about him. Pass me that camera off the table over there, would you?" Roxanne brought it over, an old Nikon SLR with a big portrait lens. Ely took it and told her to go stand by the wall facing the windows.

While Roxanne got positioned, Ely opened the bottom drawer of her paint cabinet and retrieved a special lens with a circular cut-out on the side, which she attached to the end of the portrait lens. The cut-out contained a precision mirror assembly allowing her to aim the camera straight ahead, but shoot subjects off to one side. She'd used it back in her portraits-for-money days to capture bratty kids who didn't want their picture taken. Great on nude beaches, too.

Ready to go, Ely backed her chair away from the easel and turned to face Roxanne, the girl fidgeting now, Ben telling her to relax, she was gonna love having her portrait painted.

Ely made a few practiced adjustments to the camera, then said, "Okay, young lady, now Ben is right. I want you to relax. All we're after here is a few preliminary poses. Casual stuff to give me a sense of how I'm going to paint you." She snugged her eye to the viewfinder and took a couple of shots, saying, "Hunter here tells me you're going into environmental studies."

"Yes, at Dalhousie."

The kid was blushing now, skittish as hell, but it didn't matter. Ely wasn't interested in shooting her yet, couldn't even see her in the viewfinder. She said, "Roxanne, honey, shift this way a bit now, would you, please?" Pointing left with her thumb, watching for Ben in the viewfinder. He was standing by the east wall with that stupid grin on his face, dressed in his usual attire, blue jeans and a plaid shirt, sandals over black socks, thin hair a mess. *Jesus Christ*, Ely thought, *will these old hippies never grow up*? She said, "Okay, kiddo, right there," as Ben appeared in the viewfinder. "Perfect." She grabbed about a dozen shots of the man, taking her time, catching subtle shifts in his mood as he watched Roxanne strike different poses, the girl having fun now.

When she had what she wanted, Ely detached the cut-out lens and said to Roxanne, "Okay, sweetie, now grab that stool over there and sit your butt down." Roxanne did, and Ely saw how she was going to paint her. "Good. Now turn your head. Other way. Excellent." She shot a bunch of variations, then rested the camera in her lap. "Okay, gang, I need you out of here. I want to finish my eagle while I still have the light." She said, "Roxanne, I'm going to need you back here tomorrow after your shift. I'll sit you down, get a few quick sketches done, then you can be on your way. If the weekend works for you, we'll get started on the painting."

Roxanne thanked her, Ben grinned, and Ely cringed inside. She was getting ready to shatter a dear friend's heart...but it had to be done.

When her guests were at the door, Ely shouted, "And Hunter. Stay the hell home, you hear? I want to do my best work for your friend, and I can't do that with you gawking over my shoulder the entire time."

* * *

The next afternoon, as planned, Ely sat Roxanne in the light of the west-facing windows and sketched her in charcoal, changing her position for each of three drawings. Roxanne felt awkward at first, being stared at like that, but Ely was so interesting and funny, she soon relaxed. Thinking it was the right thing to do, she tried to sit statue-still while Ely worked and Ely kept making jokes about it, saying things like, "Will you for God's sake loosen up, child? It's a sketch, not a firing squad." Or, "Are your ears cold, girlie? 'Cause if they're not, I need you to drop those shoulders."

Roxanne was amazed at how fast the artist worked—three sketches in an hour-and-a-half—and how little it seemed to matter how carefully she held a pose. Once Ely'd made her feel at home, she'd laughed and fidgeted the entire time. And when she saw the finished sketches, she could hardly believe her eyes. "Ely, these are incredible. I'd love to get them framed for Gram."

Ely said, "These are just roughs, honey," and fanned them out on the coffee table. "To get an idea how we're going to sit you. Which one's your favorite?"

Roxanne studied each in turn, then touched the second in the series, a charcoal snapshot of herself on a high wooden stool, legs crossed, face angled toward the windows. She said, "I love them all—but this one's my favorite."

Ely smiled. "Me, too, kiddo. You've got a good eye." She scooped up the sketch and clipped it to the easel. "You like surprises?"

"Good ones, yeah."

"There's a twenty-dollar bill on the kitchen counter. I want you to run down to the boutique and get us each one of those delicious Häagen-Dazs treats. The salted caramel ones on a stick."

Roxanne laughed. "Did Ben get you started on those?"

"Other way around. Now scoot. Give me half an hour."

* * *

Ely was just finishing up when Roxanne tapped at the apartment door. Ely hollered, "One sec," and draped a sheet over the sketch. Now she said, "Okay," and Roxanne breezed in with a frozen treat in her hand. Ely said, "Get that out of the box for me, would you, sweetheart?"

Roxanne opened the package and handed the snack to Ely, who dug right in, saying, "Where's yours?"

Roxanne gave her a guilty grin. "I couldn't wait."

Ely belted out that big laugh of hers, then tugged the sheet off the easel. When Roxanne saw what she'd done, she gave the artist a huge hug.

"Oh, Ely, that's *perfect*."

Ben was in the sketch now, standing next to Roxanne, the angle of her head giving the impression she was turning to face him, happy he was there.

"Ely, you are so *sneaky*. How did you pull this off?"

Ely showed her the cheater lens. "Neat, huh?"

"Very."

Ely said, "What day is it, kitten?"

"Friday."

"Are we good to go for the weekend?"

Roxanne nodded. "I'm a free agent."

"Tomorrow morning, then. Ten o'clock?"

"I'll be here. What should I wear?"

"Whatever your heart desires. But colors, so the old man doesn't make you look drab. I should paint him in the buff for giving me such a hard time."

Roxanne laughed. "I think he's just shy. I'm sure he's going to love it when it's done."

Ely did her best to smile, thinking, *That's not really the reaction I'm going for,* and accepted the girl's warm peck on the cheek.

* * *

Roxanne left Ely's apartment and thumbed the elevator call button. She couldn't remember feeling so excited. Ely was like some mythic sorceress, her ability to capture a person's essence almost magical in its purity. She'd sensed Ely's power even before she set eyes on the woman that first day with Ben, hearing her big voice bellow, *"It's open,"* and then walking down that long corridor to the studio, the walls adorned with the most amazing portraits she'd ever seen, some dating as far back as the fifties. Women, mostly—one holding a wine glass, another laughing, another on the verge of tears— but a few men too, some of them nude. Each suspended in a moment that wasn't always flattering, but sparkled with authenticity. Something about the process—sitting still like that, those keen eyes on you, the artist's probing questions teasing away the mask—made it impossible to disguise what was in your secret heart.

She couldn't wait to see what Ely found inside of her. Pain, she was certain, her grandfather so recently passed, her and Gram facing some tough decisions about the future. Love. Hope. Fear. Joy at having these wonderful people come into her life when she needed them most: Ben, Ely, even Ben's kooky high school buddies. It made her grateful she'd been raised by her grandparents, the experience teaching her that old folks weren't simply spent husks waiting to die, but loving, vibrant, intelligent human beings with so much to offer anyone perceptive enough to see it. In high school, she'd ended friendships with some of her peers because of their short-sighted attitudes, a couple of them coming right out and saying how creepy it must've been being raised by her grandparents. Thinking about it now, she realized she had more meaningful relationships with residents here at the Center than she did with people her own age.

The elevator arrived and Roxanne stepped aboard. Facing the control panel, she considered stopping off on nine to visit Ben. But Gram would be expecting her, and she decided to look in on him Monday after her shift.

* * *

Roxanne said, "So how did you and Ben meet?"

Ely eyed her around the edge of the canvas. There was a smudge of arterial-red oil paint on her nose, almost shocking in the Saturday morning sunlight, and Roxanne wondered if she should say something about it. But over the course of the forty or so minutes she'd been posing, she'd gotten the sense Ely had slipped into a sort of waking trance, those sharp eyes ticking back and forth between canvas and subject, and she didn't want to risk breaking the spell. Ely had told her from the outset talking was fine, even a certain amount of movement. But she decided to hold her tongue. Besides, it was kind of funny, this incredibly talented artist peering at her with laser-like intensity over her horn rims—with a big smear of clown paint on her nose.

In answer to Roxanne's question, Ely said, "He wanted to be an artist. I rented an apartment downtown over a music store his mother worked at. Beautiful woman. She brought me a stack of his pencil drawings one day and said he wanted to meet me. Ben was around fifteen at the time, I think. Maybe younger. Handsome boy. Talented, too. But a southpaw, always dragging his hand through the work. Anyway, we became fast friends." She cackled. "Though I think I was more of a father figure to him. Taught him how to use power tools. Worked the ass off him, too. He helped build my lake house in the Gatineaus." Ely squinted now. "Lift your chin for me, sweetheart. Bit more…there."

"What about his art?"

Ely cackled again. "Found his pecker and lost interest. Endless parade of wide-eyed hippie chicks. We had the place on the lake finished by then, and I'd pick him up whenever I was in town, him and his latest squeeze. The kid was some kind of magician, getting a new one to fall for him every few weeks." She laughed. "Free love."

Roxanne said, "I never would've guessed. He told me he never married. Just buried himself in the work and lost track of time. Shame. He would've made a great dad."

Ely put the brush down and Roxanne could see the trance was broken. "I think you're right," the artist said — with a trace of melancholy, Roxanne thought. "He would've made a wonderful dad."

"Did he ever come close?"

"To marriage? No. To loving someone enough *to* marry her? Hell yes, and then some. But it didn't work out."

"How come?"

"They were young. And Ben was...damaged."

Roxanne said, "What do you mean?"

"Dismal family life. You know. Angry, distant father. Violent man. Used his fists on Ben and the mother. Poor kid. I guess he thought that was what love was and decided never to trust it."

"What was she like?"

"His mother?"

"No, the girl. The one he fell in love with."

Ely thought, *A lot like you.* "Sweet as hell. Tall. Beautiful. Very mature. But it got so Ben couldn't stand to have her out of his sight. They were kids, mind you — sixteen, seventeen when they met — and 'love' at that age is madness to begin with. But he got crazy jealous if she even glanced at another boy. And he kept coming up with different ways to make her prove her feelings for him, causing all kinds of upset. Wore the girl out. When she finally broke it off, I thought he was actually going to die of a broken heart."

"What about all those other girls?"

Ely laughed, a blunt, humorless sound. "Playthings. They came after. More than a few fell for him pretty hard. Sweet girls, too, some of them. But it was just never the same for him after that first one. I sketched them together once; I may still have it around here somewhere. Anyway, I think he decided losing his girl was some kind of karmic payback—for what I don't know—and he withdrew. He was in med school by then and just gave himself to the work."

Roxanne said, "That is so sad."

"It's just life, kitten." Ely stretched now, saying, "Okay, enough of this nonsense. Let's get you back in position." Roxanne resumed her pose and Ely said, "Turn your hips a little to the right—there, that's it. Now relax."

They were quiet for a time now, the only sounds the dab and whisk of the artist's brush, and the muted chatter of a radio in another room.

As the minutes ticked past, Roxanne felt herself drifting into a trancelike state of her own, her thoughts turning to Russ now. How right they were for each other. Last night had been Gram's bridge night, and because she owned a car, it fell to her to pick up some of her fellow players. Taking advantage of the empty house, Roxanne had invited Russ over for dinner. She'd planned on making spaghetti, but Russ had shown up a half-hour early with two big bags of takeout from Al's.

Seafood this time. Atlantic salmon and pan-seared tilapia, with sautéed mussels and crab-stuffed mushrooms for appetizers.

She smiled to herself now, remembering their first kiss and how delicious it had been, in spite of tasting like a tide pool...

Ely was saying something now, and Roxanne tuned her in.

* * *

Ely said, "Okay, darlin', I need a break." She'd been puzzling over how best to tell Roxanne about Ben's disease, and decided the kindest approach would be to just come straight out with it. The kid deserved to know. She said, "My back's killing me."

Roxanne said, "Sure," and hopped off the stool.

Watching her move, Ely said, "If I tried a stunt like that, I'd shatter like a clay pot."

"I hope I'm half as spry as you when I'm *eighty*," Roxanne said, stretching her long body, "never mind a hundred-and-two."

Laughing, Ely backed her chair away from the easel. She said, "Why don't you sit at the table and I'll fix us some tea."

Roxanne was on her feet in a flash. "You relax. I've got this."

Ely watched her scoot into the kitchen, then parked her chair at the dinner table. Roxanne joined her a few minutes later with the tea. Ely took a sip and told her it was delicious. Then she said, "There's something I want to talk to you about, sweetie. It's kind of delicate, so I want you to bear with me. I've known Ben for a long time, and I love him like a son. And I know you care about him too."

"I do. Very much."

Ely nodded. "Now please, don't take this the wrong way, but I can see Ben has become a kind of substitute for your grandfather, and—"

"That's true, Ely. I was just thinking about that this morning."

"And I'm not saying there's anything wrong with that. It's perfectly natural. But here's the thing. I think—no, I'm quite certain—Ben's doing the same thing with you."

Roxanne said, "How so?" then appeared stricken, saying, "Oh, God, he didn't have a child who died, did he?"

"No, nothing like that. It's complicated. When he's in his right mind, you're *like* the child he never had. You bring out a paternal instinct in the man that's wonderful to see. In that way, you're filling a hole in his life he didn't realize existed, and he loves you for it."

Roxanne smiled. Then the smile faltered. "But when he's *not* in his right mind..."

"That's when it gets complicated."

"But it hasn't been that long since the doctor made him stop taking the pills that were messing him up. Maybe he just needs a little more time—"

Ely silenced her with an upraised hand, saying, "I'm going to tell you something now, Roxanne. Something I should probably keep to myself. But I like you, and I think you deserve to know. Ben's problem isn't his pills." She touched her temple with a bent finger. "It's up here."

"What do you mean?"

Ely said, "Ben has Alzheimer's disease," and instantly regretted it. Tears sprang to Roxanne's eyes, and she seemed to shrink inside her skin. Ely took her hand. "But it's early on yet, honey, so most of the time he's fine."

"But he *invented* a drug that treats the disease, right? If he takes it, he'll be fine. Right? Isn't he taking it?"

"He tried to, but he's deathly allergic. If he'd been alone when he swallowed that capsule, he'd be dead now."

Roxanne only stared at her, shell-shocked.

Ely said, "I'm telling you this because I don't want to see you get hurt." Roxanne gave her an ironic look, blowing air through her nose, and Ely said, "I realize this part's hurtful. It tore me up when he told me. But if you want to continue spending time with him, you need to know what you're up against."

* * *

It took Ely three days to finish the painting: one more sitting with Roxanne on Sunday, then day and night from memory and the photographs, pushing the oils as fast as they'd go. When it was done, she called Ben and told him she needed to see him right away.

* * *

They were in Ely's studio, Ben on the couch, Ely by her cloth-shrouded easel, hunched in her motorized chair. Ben was a smart guy, and since he seemed in his right mind at the moment, Ely decided to confront him head on.

"Can't you see what you're doing here, Hunter? You're four times the kid's age and you're behaving like she's your girlfriend."

Infuriated, Ben got to his feet. "This bullshit again? From *you*? You must have been talking to those idiots Quinn and Wilder. Because what you're saying is absurd. I know I'm not her *boy*friend, Ely. Jesus, I can't believe this shit—"

"Just *listen* to me, would you? I saw how you behaved around girls when you were a teenager, many times, so I know what I'm talking about. She loves you, there's no question about that. But as a *friend*, goddammit...and as a stand-in for her grandfather. I'm not saying that part of it's healthy, but it is understandable. You just sort of stepped into his shoes. A wise old guy who loves her and gives her guidance."

"I get that, Ely, and I'm okay with it. I couldn't be happier, in fact. But this other nonsense, what you're suggesting—to be frank, it's the product of a sick mind."

"I agree with you, Ben. It *is* the product of a sick mind. Yours."

"You're not suggesting I'd ever—"

"Not for a second. I'm not talking about that kind of sick. I know you'd never lay a hand on her." Though she hadn't been certain until she'd spoken to Roxanne.

"I can see it's not about that." She angled the easel to face him now, tugging off the screening cloth. Ben glanced at the painting beneath it and averted his gaze, cheeks flushing crimson. Ely said, "I want you to look at this, Hunter."

He kept his eyes averted. "I saw it. I asked you to paint *her*, not both of—"

"Look at the fucking *painting*."

Ben did, and Ely saw bewilderment narrow his gaze. He shrugged, saying, "What's your point?" But he looked away again.

"My *point*—look at the painting, Ben." He did. "My point," Ely said, tapping the canvas with a blunt fingernail, "is this is *not* how you see yourself when you're with the girl. It's not all the time. Just when you're having one of your spells. But it's often enough to hurt and confuse her."

Ben said, "You're not making any sense," and turned away, ready to leave.

"Ben—"

"No, Ely. This is bullshit and I won't hear another word of it." At the door he said, "And if you bring it up again, you and I are done."

Then he was gone.

Ely sighed and repositioned the easel. After a quick inspection of her work, she dug out her palette and oils. She didn't like the way the sun was flaring off the wall behind Ben's head.

* * *

Roxanne said, "Ely, this is so beautiful."

The artist smiled, angling the canvas to better catch the light. "Ain't it, though?"

"Has Ben seen it yet?"

Ely nodded. "Yesterday."

"And?"

"He hates it. I told him why I did it and he walked out on me."

Roxanne's pleased smile vanished. "Then you know what, Ely? Maybe we're wrong. Maybe if we give it a little more time, it'll just…"

"Go away?"

Roxanne nodded.

"Do you really believe that?"

"I guess not. If anything, it's gotten worse." She sank into a squat beside Ely's chair. "Do you think I should stop spending time with him?"

Ely took the girl's hand and gave it a squeeze. "Much as I hate to say it, it may come to that. But I've got one more trick up my sleeve."

"Tell me."

"It's pretty radical. If you're not up for it, I'll understand."

"Ely, at this point I'm willing to try anything."

"All right. Here's what I think you should do."

SEVEN

Saturday, July 8

HUNCHED OVER AN iPAD on Ben's couch, Quinn said, "So Benji, what are you guys going to see?" Wilder was in the kitchen, scouting up a beer chaser for the brownie he'd just eaten. Quinn had wolfed one too, and was just beginning to catch a buzz.

Ben came out of the bathroom adjusting his tie. "That new Tarantino film. I forget what it's called."

Quinn made a few brisk finger-strokes across the iPad screen. "*I Love You, Charlie Bronson*? The *zombie* flick? Should you really be taking a minor to an R-rated bloodbath?"

She's almost nineteen, you moron, and she loves Tarantino. I do, too. The guy's a weird genius. Anyway, it was her idea."

Quinn shook his head. "You should be arrested."

"Kiss my ass. Is my tie on straight?"

"You should be more concerned whether your *head's* on straight."

"Prick."

"Jesus, no, Ben, I didn't mean it that way. I meant taking a kid to a—"

Ben grinned. "Gotcha."

"You can kiss *my* ass."

Ben said, "The tie?"

"The tie's fine." Quinn flipped the iPad around to show Ben. "What about this one? More suitable, don't you think?"

Ben leaned in to view the glowing screen: movie listings for the Center's three-theater Cineplex. Seeing the one Quinn had highlighted, he snorted. "A Pixar film? Really? You trying to make a point here, Quinn? Because there's a perfectly good one on the top of your head."

Laughing, Quinn closed the iPad. "I'm just saying. If you're going to rob the cradle, you should probably consider a more age-appropriate film."

Wilder came into the room now, chugging a beer. He sat next to Quinn, burped prodigiously, and slammed the empty onto the coffee table. Glancing at Ben, he said, "You're out of beer. Want a brownie?"

"No thank you. I don't want Roxanne seeing me half out of my head on pot." He checked his watch. "Now I need you two gone. I'm meeting her in the lobby in ten minutes."

Wilder leaned closer to Quinn to say, "She's already seen him *all* the way out his head," and Quinn couldn't help himself. He laughed. The sativa always made him giddy.

Ben shot them a dirty look and Quinn immediately felt guilty. He wanted to apologize, but he couldn't stop laughing, and when Wilder started snickering, he lost it completely.

Ben was holding the apartment door open now, no sign of amusement on his face. When they skulked past him into the hallway, *still* laughing, Ben said, "Cruel bastards," so softly Quinn almost didn't hear him.

But he did.

He turned now, trying to compose himself enough to apologize. But the door was already closed, the deadbolt running home with a deliberate *snap*.

Feeling like a fool, Quinn started down the hall, Wilder still chuckling behind him. In the elevator on the way down, Quinn said, "That was really shitty of us."

Grinning, Wilder said, "Maybe. But that's what we do. We mock. It's what we've always done. That old crybaby does it too, when it suits him."

"Yeah, but sometimes…"

"Sometimes what?"

"Sometimes a line gets crossed. You know what I mean?"

Wilder said, "Maybe. But on the bright side, I haven't seen the man that clear-headed in days."

"There's that," Quinn said, poking the button for the lobby. They were headed for the rec center now to shoot some pool. Grudge match. Last time they played, Wilder had fleeced him for thirty bucks.

Quinn heard the crinkle of tinfoil, and turned to see Wilder unwrapping the last of the brownies. Holding them out on his palm, Wilder said, "One more for the road?"

Quinn scooped one up. "Don't mind if I do."

* * *

Ben spotted her right away, standing by the entrance with a casually dressed boy of about her age. For an eyeblink, he thought he recognized the kid, but as he closed the distance he changed his mind. Just a trick of the light.

Roxanne smiled when she saw him—a little apprehensively, Ben thought—and as she turned to face him, he realized she was holding hands with her companion. He returned her smile, thinking, *Oh, my, what have we here?* She hadn't told him she was seeing someone.

Still smiling, Ben offered his hand to the young man and thought he saw an expectant tension drop out of Roxanne's shoulders, her previously guarded smile more genuine now. He said, "Hi, there," and shook the kid's hand. "I'm Ben Hunter, and that's my date you're holding hands with."

The kid dropped Roxanne's hand like it was a dead rat and Ben laughed, saying, "I'm *kidd*ing. For God's sake, son, I'm only kidding."

The kid laughed now too, taking Roxanne's hand again, saying, "Oh, okay. Pleased to meet you, sir. I'm Russ."

Ben thought, *Russ*, and felt that twitch of familiarity again. He said, "Have we met?" and Roxanne jumped in.

"Uh, Ben, we should probably get going. The movie starts in fifteen minutes."

Ben said, "Don't worry, hon. The theater's only a five-minute walk." Smiling again, he said, "So I take it the two of you are an item?" and watched Roxanne's face turn flame red. He loved that about her. Wore her heart right out there on her sleeve.

Blushing himself, Russ glanced at Roxanne and said, "I hope so, sir."

Mock stern now, Ben said, "Well, fair warning, chum. Break her heart, you'll have me to answer to."

The kid just nodded.

Ben said, "So what's up? Are you joining us this evening, Russ?"

"No, sir, I'm just dropping her, Roxanne...I'm just dropping her off. Her grandmother needed the car to-night, and I didn't want her taking the bus. I'll be back at ten-thirty to pick her up."

"That's very nice of you, son. But listen, why *don't* you join us?"

"I'd love to, sir, but—"

Ben said, "Please, Russ, enough with the *sir*. I feel old enough as it is. Just call me Ben."

"Okay, Ben." He grinned. "I'd love to join you guys, but I've got a band practice tonight."

Ben put his hand on the kid's shoulder. "A fellow musician." He grinned at Roxanne, saying, "I'm liking this cat more by the minute." And to Russ, "What instrument do you play?"

"Drums."

"*Drums.* A man after my own heart."

"You play, sir—uh, Ben?"

"Bought my first kit with paper-route money when I was twelve. Ludwigs. Four-piece red-sparkle with a 'Squeak' King pedal. Who's your favorite drummer?"

"John Bonham. Hands down the best that ever lived."

Laughing, Ben said, "Roxanne, you have my permission to marry this boy." And to Russ, "What's the name of your band?"

"Conduct Unbecoming. We were Inflatable Amusements for a while, but too many people took it the wrong way. We're a three-piece: bass, guitar, drums."

"That's always been my favorite configuration. Love the name, by the way. Both of them, actually. What kind of stuff do you play?"

"Classic Rock. Hardcore."

"Excellent."

Checking her watch, Roxanne said, "Okay, boys, I can see you'd like to stand here all night talking music, but it's time to go. The lineups are going to be brutal, and I need time to pee and buy Twizzlers."

Ben told her they were going to a theater tailored to old folks, so he didn't think there'd be much of a turn-out for a movie about dead people. Russ laughed, gave Roxanne a peck on the lips and said he had to run too, he'd see her back here at ten-thirty. Then he was gone.

Ben stuck out his elbow. "Shall we?"

Picking up on the emerging ritual, Roxanne said, "We most certainly shall," and took his arm.

* * *

Roxanne couldn't be happier. Part of Ely's strategy for making Ben see her for who she really was included keeping Russ as far out of the picture as possible. But when Russ offered to drive her to the Center tonight, she decided to take a chance, reasoning if Ben saw them together, really *saw* them, it might be enough to snap him out of his fantasy world for good. And so far, it appeared to be working like a charm.

As they strolled to the Cineplex in lavender dusk light, Roxanne told him a little more about Russ—carefully avoiding how they met—saying she'd attend-ed a band practice the evening before ("They're great, but really *loud*."), and that by sheer coincidence, Russ would be going to school in Nova Scotia too, taking the undergrad music program at Acadia University, only an hour's drive from Halifax. The whole band was going.

It was at this point she feared she was losing Ben, the man sporting that dazed expression again as they en-tered the shopping concourse.

But now he looked her in the eyes and said how romantic he thought it was, the two of them ending up so close to each other for school, like it was meant to be. He said, "I'm happy for you, Roxanne. You deserve a nice boy like Russ." And for the first time ever, he touched her, resting his hand on her shoulder for as long as it took him to say, "I was just thinking how much I'm going to miss you when you're gone."

Roxanne wanted to tell him she'd Skype him every week, and spend time with him during her visits home. But they'd reached the Cineplex now and she'd been right. The place was packed.

Seeming distressed, Ben told her to take care of her ablutions, he'd grab the tickets and Twizzlers and meet her in front of the theater. By the time she got there, the opening credits were already rolling.

The movie was great, in places so terrifying Roxanne actually cried out. At one point, a morbidly obese zombie burst through a stage floor to sink its teeth into the ankle of an exotic dancer, using its massive weight to pluck her off the stripper pole and drag her kicking and screaming into the space beneath the stage. The attack was so sudden, Roxanne shrieked and seized Ben's hand, clutching it as hard as she could until the scene cut to daylight, offering a brief respite from the action.

She tried to take her hand back then—recalling what Ely had told her about physical contact—but Ben tightened his grip. Not uncomfortably; just enough to let her know he didn't want to break the connection. She considered insisting, but it seemed harmless enough—and now an elderly zombie in a gore-drenched nightgown dropped out of a tree onto the heroine's back, cocking its jaws to savage the girl's neck. The audience gasped, unable to believe the main character was about to join the ranks of the living dead. Then the camera cut to the zombie's mouth, toothlessly gumming the girl's skin, and everyone laughed. The heroine flipped the dead thing off her back, stomped its brains into the tarmac, and jacked a round into her assault rifle.

It wasn't long before Roxanne had to pee again, and she tugged her hand free, telling Ben she'd be right back. Excitement went straight to her bladder, a fact Russ had already picked up on, necking with her in the front seat of his Tesla.

On her way back, she spotted Ben on a bench in the lobby, staring at a panel of flashing lights over the concession booth. Concerned, she sat next to him and said his name. When he didn't respond, she touched his arm and he turned to face her. Smiling, he said, "Roxanne. Hi, sweetie."

"Are you okay?"

"Yeah, I'm fine. I decided to hit the bathroom too, but on the way out I got short of breath. Happens sometimes. Figured I'd sit here a minute."

Relieved—seeing him sitting here alone with that vacant look on his face had shaken her—Roxanne said, "Want to just head home?"

He raised an eyebrow. "And miss seeing how Fiona 'Remington' Faraday takes out the head ghoul?" He grinned. "I really don't think so."

He stood, offering his arm. "Shall we?"
Roxanne laughed. "We most certainly shall."

* * *

For the balance of the film, Ben sat staring at the seat in front of him, trying to puzzle out how he'd ended up in the lobby. He knew he'd lost touch for a while; his last recollection before Roxanne spotted him out there was of a zombie dropping out of a tree. And he wasn't kidding himself; he knew he had Alzheimer's disease. But he was still a physician, and while the condition terrified him, it was also fascinating. And what better way to study a disease than to have it oneself? Except the very organ required to understand it—to understand *any*thing—was the one most critically affected. He'd tried to connect the dots before, many times, wracking his brain for the details of those lost seconds or minutes or hours, but he'd always come up short. And the bits he *did* remember were just...there, and often startling in their clarity.

It made him think of a train ride he'd taken in Europe in the eighties, on his way to a conference in Bern. The lights had gone out as they entered a series of tunnels, raising murmurs of alarm—then they were in daylight again, the contrast shocking to the senses. That pattern of light and dark had repeated several times before they broke out onto open terrain and the lights came on to stay.

Searching his memory after his spells was a lot like that, extended periods of blackness intercut by almost blinding moments of clarity.

Pondering it awakened an ache at the base of his skull, and as he left the mall, he was startled to find a beautiful girl walking next to him. At first he thought she was trying to pass him on the lockstone path, and he slowed to let her by. Then she said, "Ben, are you okay?" and he knew right away who she was. He smiled and said he was fine. Strangely, it felt as if he hadn't seen the girl in eons. Which was nonsense, of course. They'd just seen a movie together, the premiere of *Butch Cassidy and the Sundance Kid*.

She smiled now and took his arm, and they walked together under an indigo sky in a place he'd never seen before.

* * *

At the elevators in the lobby, Roxanne said, "Russ won't be here for another forty minutes, but you should go ahead up anyway, Ben. You look tired. I've got my reader, I'll be fine down here."

"Wait down here alone? Nonsense." Ben pressed the UP button. "That gives us just enough time to catch an episode of *South Park*, which starts in exactly..." He checked his watch. "Nine-and-a-half minutes."

"Sounds fun."

The elevator arrived and Roxanne followed him into the vacant car. He stared at the control panel for a long beat, then Roxanne pressed 9 and the doors slid shut. Ben said, "Nine, right." Then: "Who's Russ?"

Oh, no. "He's my ride."

Ben nodded. "So what did you think of the film?"

"Pretty wild," Roxanne said, hoping he was kidding about Russ.

"My favorite part was the knife fight."

"Knife fight?" At least a hundred zombies had been slain with everything from chopsticks to machetes, but none had fought back with a knife.

"Yeah. Remember? When Butch Cassidy says, 'Not until me and Harvey get the rules straightened out'."

Butch Cassidy?

The doors opened on the ninth floor and Ben turned left into the hallway. Roxanne said, "Ben, it's this way," and knew he was gone. Knew she'd have to go through with Ely's plan, even though the prospect scared the hell out of her. And she knew if it didn't work, she'd never be able to see Ben Hunter again. It was just too painful, for both of them.

Which made it worth a try.

She felt a fresh glimmer of hope when they got to Ben's door and he stopped without being told, punching in the key code with practiced confidence.

But that hope was shattered a moment later in the foyer.

Ben hung his jacket on a hook by the entryway mirror and turned to face her, a distant, almost dreamy glaze in his eyes. Grinning, he said, "Know what I was thinking about this morning?"

"No."

"I was thinking about the day I asked you to go steady. I was so afraid you'd say no, I could hardly breathe. I had my grandfather's ring. Remember what you said?"

Crestfallen, Roxanne said, "Tell me," and moved closer. Kissing close.

Ben said, "Uh," and shuffled back a step, hands pressed to his temples now, as if to prevent them from splitting. "Uh, you said…"

Closing the distance again, Roxanne undid the top button of her blouse, her eyes never leaving Ben's. By the third button, he'd begun to tremble, but not with excitement. It was like watching a man shake himself apart from the inside, a convulsion of opposing forces.

In a voice that shook with alarm, he said, "What's going on?" and stumbled back another step, almost losing his balance.

Eyes stinging, Roxanne undid another button. "Isn't this what you want?"

"Roxanne, *no*. Of *course* not. Why…?"

Taking Ben's arm, Roxanne turned him to face the mirror, standing beside him now, locking eyes with his reflection.

She said, "Do you see yourself?"

At first there was no response, and Roxanne held his gaze in the mirror, his reddening eyes locked on hers. Then he looked away, first at the reflected image of the room behind him…then, more gradually, at himself, eyes widening as they ticked from the deep seams in his forehead to the pronounced furrows bracketing his mouth to the loose wattle of flesh beneath his chin.

His lips trembled as he said, "Yes."

"Who are you?"

"Ben Hunter."

"And do you see me?"

He nodded.

"Who am I?"

"Roxanne. You're my friend, Roxanne Austen."

Buttoning her blouse now, Roxanne said, "Do you see *us*?"

Ben nodded, saying, "Yes, sweetheart, I do. I really do."

They stood there a while, seeing each other in the mirror.

Then Roxanne said, "Ben, I should be going. Russ'll be here soon, and I need to run down to my locker before he arrives. Are you going to be okay?"

Glancing at his watch, Ben said, "Well, you made me miss the beginning of *South Park*," and Roxanne laughed so explosively it hurt her throat. He said, "Thank you, Roxanne," and pulled her into a fatherly hug. "It's been so confusing. I was furious at Ely and the guys for even bringing it up. I thought they were trying to make our friendship into something dirty...but they were right. They were only trying to help."

Roxanne nodded in his embrace.

He released her now, nudging her out to arm's length. "This wasn't your idea, was it."

"No."

"Ely?"

"Uh huh."

"She's a crafty old witch, isn't she?"

"She really is."

He opened the apartment door. "That took some real courage," he said. "Shocked the hell out of me, but you made your point." He put his hand on her shoulder. "But listen, sweetheart. I'm sick. There's no getting around it. Some days I'm fine. Others, it's hour-by-hour, even minute-by-minute. Like tonight. I remember punching in the code at the apartment door, but I don't remember getting off the elevator."

"I understand."

"What I'm saying is, even in spite of what you did here tonight, I might be right back where I started before I close the door behind you."

Roxanne said, "Maybe. But maybe not." She walked him back to the mirror. "Besides, I can always remind you." She popped up on tiptoes to kiss him on the cheek, then moved into the hallway. "Nite, Ben. See you tomorrow for lunch?"

Ben said, "I'll have to check my schedule," and laughed. "Our usual table?"

"Twelve-thirty sharp."

She smiled and scooted down the hallway.

And with the abruptness of a lightning strike, Ben thought, *That's the girl I'm going to marry.* He watched her till she boarded the elevator, then closed the door without locking it. He toed off his shoes and settled into the La-Z-Boy, hugging a pillow to his chest. He stared at the blank TV for a while, seeing their Hawaiian honey-moon in the blazing Technicolor of dementia. Until sleep claimed him, deep and dreamless, a dark refuge from his disease.

* * *

Ely squinted at the blank canvas, an elegant composition taking shape in her mind. She'd taped some faded Polaroids to the edge of the canvas, shots she'd taken decades ago in New Mexico: a trio of domestic geese; a primitive hay wagon; different angles on an aging adobe ranch house. Her idea was to combine these elements into—

There was a knock at the door now, so tentative Ely almost missed it. She glanced at the mantle clock—4:06 PM, too late for the pharmacy tech—then hollered, "Who is it?"

"Ely, it's Roxanne. Can I come in?"

"Of course. It's unlocked."

Ely angled her chair to face the hallway, eager to see Roxanne's smiling mug. She looked forward to the kid's visits now, her presence a ray of sunshine in the often lonely confines of the apartment.

But there was no smile today. The girl looked puffy and tired.

Ely said, "Sweetheart, what's wrong?"

Roxanne plunked onto the couch, gathering her legs beneath her. She tried to speak, but she was too busy biting back tears.

Ely said, "Is it Ben?"

Roxanne nodded, a single tear skating down her cheek to land on her jeans.

"You tried what we talked about?"

Another nod. "Last night."

"And it didn't work?"

Managing a thin smile, Roxanne said, "Actually, it worked great." She cuffed her eyes dry. "I thought we'd made a solid breakthrough." She went on to describe the encounter in front of the mirror and how hopeful she'd been, telling Russ about it on the drive home. "But I met him for lunch today and he was worse than ever, going on about our plans for after school, asking me if I wanted to go to the Centennial parade on the weekend."

"That was in nineteen-sixty-seven."

"I know. I looked it up."

"So that's it, then," Ely said, heartsick for this precious child.

"I guess it is," Roxanne said. "But I've decided to hang in anyway, Ely, now that I understand what's going on. It's not his fault, and it's not all the time. And when he's lucid, we have the best conversations. I learn something new every time we're together. He's brilliant."

"That he is."

"And when he gets lost...well, it's harmless, right?"

Ely nodded. "I suppose so."

"So I'll just guide him through it. I'll be moving to Halifax in the fall anyway. No reason to chicken out now."

As if viewing the scene in slow motion, Ely watched Roxanne change positions on the couch, angling to the right now to lie on her side, head coming to rest on a shaggy pillow, hair pooling in artful whorls around her face —

Ely said, "Jesus H. Christ," and spun her chair so quickly she almost knocked over the easel.

Roxanne said, "Ely, are you okay?" and started to get up.

"*No,*" Ely said. "Don't move from that spot."

In spite of her bewilderment, the girl complied, sinking back onto her side, that worry line showing again.

Ely stared at her a moment longer, solidifying the image in her mind, then motored over to an antique chest with a stack of shallow drawers. She opened the bottom drawer and began thumbing through a bunch of old sketches, casting back in her mind to an autumn day many years ago...to a teenage Ben showing up at the lake house with this girl, looking like he'd been clapped on the back of the head with a plank. It had been Ely's idea to sketch them, and she remembered feeling compelled to do so, the sight of them strolling hand-in-hand up the walkway in lush October sunshine one of the most stunning she'd ever witnessed. They had positively *glowed* with the heat of young love, and Ely wanted to capture it in case she never saw it again. And she never had. Not like that.

She ran the drawer closed and opened the next one up, wondering why she hadn't twigged to this before now. There was a very good reason Ben had fixated on Roxanne and not someone else.

Ah, here it is.

She eased the pastel out of a plastic sleeve and felt the breath catch in her throat, these two gorgeous kids stretched out on a worn leather couch, Ben shirtless on his back with his face angled into the room, the girl tucked under his arm with her head on his chest, hair strewn in golden swirls around her placid face. The date beneath Ely's signature was 1968.

Sixty years. My God...

She ran the drawer shut, placed the drawing face-down on her lap, and returned to her spot across the coffee table from Roxanne. She said, "You can sit up now, darling."

Roxanne did, her gaze fixed on the overturned sketch. "What's that?"

"Remember the girl I told you about? The one who broke Ben's heart?"

"Yes."

"Well, I think you might know her."

Ely flipped the sketch over and gave it to Roxanne, unsurprised by her startled gasp.

Wide-eyed, Roxanne said, "Is this who I think it is?"

"I was hoping you could tell me."

Angling the sketch toward the windows, Roxanne said, "I've only seen one picture of her at this age, in her high school yearbook. But I'm pretty sure this is Gram."

"What's her real name, sweetie?"

"Melanie Anderson."

"Yup. That's the one."

"Oh my *God*."

Roxanne was smiling now, ear-to-ear and bright as sunshine, and Ely knew what the girl was thinking. She wanted to run home right now and get the entire juicy scoop from her grandmother. But Ely had a better idea, one that might benefit all concerned.

She said, "Here's what I'm thinking. If you and your grandmother are standing right in front of the man—no warning for either of them—number one, it's going to be damned hard for him to mix the two of you up. And number two, depending on how your grandmother reacts, it might just fix this whole mess for good."

* * *

Roxanne called Ben on her way down to the lobby.

"Hello?"

"Hey, Ben."

"Hey, Roxie, what's up?"

Good, he knows it's me. "If you have plans for tomorrow morning, I need you to cancel them. Breakfast is on me. I'll pick you up in the lobby at nine.

"There's someone I want you to meet."

EIGHT

Monday, July 10

BEN WAS READY BY seven-thirty, dressed in jeans and a faded T-shirt, sandals over the executive socks on his feet. He'd stuck a Post-it note to the fridge last night after Roxanne called—*Breakfast with Rox, lobby at 0900*—but had managed to remember the arrangement on his own. He was aware of the current strategies for coping with dementia—he'd published a number of seminal papers on the subject himself—and had begun incorporating many of them into his daily routine. But on the few occasions he managed to get by without these simple aids, he felt a genuine sense of hope, even a little pride.

The phone rang at eight o'clock and Ben felt a stab of disappointment, certain it was Roxanne calling to cancel. But it was his friend and colleague, Dr. Jake Barbeau, the man he'd worked most closely with in the development of anti-aggregates. Ben was delighted to hear from him.

"Jake, what a nice surprise. How *are* you?"

"Hello, Ben, I'm well, thank you. I've been meaning to call you for quite some time now, but things have been so busy, I—"

"Put it out of your head, my friend. I remember the eighteen-hour days, catnapping on that godforsaken couch in the staff lounge. Have you set fire to that torture rack yet?"

Jake laughed. "It's all leather in there now. And we have sleep rooms."

"Is this your way of trying to entice me back into the fold?"

"If I thought you'd *come* back, I'd charter a plane."

Ben and Jake had spent two years together at the University of Toronto, ironing the kinks out of their breakthrough treatment. Those had been heady times. In addition to the life-changing deal they'd struck with Pfizer, both men had been offered lucrative positions in research and development. Jake, twenty years Ben's junior, had jumped aboard without hesitation. But Ben had opted to return to his geriatric practice, much to Jake's disappointment.

Ben said, "I'm afraid I'm past all that now. Besides, in my condition, I'd probably end up torching the place with a forgotten Bunsen burner." Jake had been the one to confirm Ben's Alzheimer's diagnosis.

"About that," Jake said. "I may have some good news. Exciting news, in fact."

Ben felt his scalp tingle. "Do tell."

"As you're well aware, Aggrecene induces a profound anaphylactic reaction in greater than one percent of patients treated. Considering the enormous population we're dealing with, that's highly significant—"

"Listen, Jake, I keep up with the literature. And no one's more conversant with the drug's allergic potential than me. So please, cut to the chase."

"Fair enough. About a month ago, we began testing a group of allergic patients with an isomer of the drug, which, so far, has failed to trigger an allergic response."

The news struck Ben like a hearty back clap. But the scientist in him said, "What about efficacy?"

"So far, so good. The patients we've been testing appear to be stabilizing. The onset of therapeutic effect is less abrupt than the original formulation, and a small number of patients experienced an actual worsening of the disease before the drug kicked in. But it's early times yet, Ben. We'll need six months to a year to be certain. But I'm optimistic. If you're interested, I can include you in the trial."

Ben said, "That would be fantastic." Yet something about it bothered him. He said, "But tell me, why'd you wait so long to let me know about this?" He flashed on the darkening cloud the disease had cast over his life in the recent past and felt a pang of resentment. "I could've *used* this stuff a month ago. The timing would've been ideal."

"I understand how you feel, my friend."

"No, Jake, you don't. And you should thank God you don't."

"Come on, Ben, you know what I mean. I waited until now to bring you in because I didn't want to engender false hope. I don't want you as a guinea pig."

Ben had more to say on the subject, but he thought of how excited Roxanne was going to be—and Ely and Wilder and Quinn and Ray—and said, "You're right, Jake. Of course, you're right. I apologize."

"No need."

"I appreciate you involving me in this, I really do. When do we start?"

"A tall-dark-handsome UPS guy will appear at your door with a box of blister packs sometime between nine and eleven this morning."

Ben laughed, thinking he'd get Quinn to wait in the apartment for the UPS guy so he could keep his breakfast date with Roxanne. He jotted *Quinn, UPS, this AM* on a Post-it note and said, "Pretty sure of yourself, aren't you. I might've answered your call this morning as Little Red Riding Hood and told you to go screw yourself."

Jake laughed now, too. "It's a chance I was willing to take. But listen, Ben. You *must* take the first dose in the presence of a physician *in* an emergency treatment facility. This is absolutely mandatory, do you understand?"

"I do."

"There's still a chance you might react. It's vanishingly small, but it exists. If I'd been thinking straight, I'd've the shipped samples to the hospital."

"I'm writing it down as we speak. And trust me, I never want to go through a reaction like that again. I won't take any chances." He stuck the note to his plastic med dispenser.

Jake said, "I've already spoken to a Doctor Skeen at the hospital there."

"The ER department head. I know him well."

"He's agreed to oversee your first dose. You have an appointment with him this afternoon at three."

"Thanks, Jake. I can't tell you how much I appreciate this."

"Millions of people around the world should be thanking *you*, my friend. That the brains behind such a marvelous discovery should be unable to benefit from it is a travesty of justice at the cosmic level."

"Thanks for saying that. But it's just bad luck."

"Okay, Ben, I have to go. Be sure to call me as soon as you know."

Ben said, "Count on it," and cradled the receiver.

Grinning at the old man in the entryway mirror, Ben let out a whoop and checked his watch.

He couldn't wait to tell Roxanne.

* * *

"Oh my God, Ben, that's amazing."

Sean Costello

He smiled. "Ain't it though? I take my test dose this afternoon."

Merging onto Bronson off Hog's Back Road, Roxanne said, "Test dose? So there's still a chance you might react?"

"Yes, but it's minimal. If I know my friend Jake, he's just being overcautious. I'm not worried, not even a little bit, so you shouldn't be either."

Roxanne said, "Tell your story walking, Mister," and Ben squinted at her, the sun in her side-window casting her in gilt-edged silhouette. It was an expression he hadn't heard in decades, and he thought, *Who used to say that?*

Now Roxanne said, "I'll make you a deal. I'll promise not to worry if you'll promise I can come along."

"To the appointment? Don't you have to work?"

"I've got the day off."

"All right then, sure. That'd be nice. It's at three o'clock."

"Okay, good," Roxanne said. "I'm trying to remember my grade twelve chemistry. Isomers... Aren't those molecules that have the same formula, but a different arrangement of atoms in space?"

Ben smiled. "Good for you. Exactly. It's a subtle change, but sometimes the effect can be significant."

"I'm so excited for you, Ben. You deserve this more than anyone."

"Well, let's just see how it goes before we bust out the champagne."

"Fingers crossed. But it'll work. You'll see."

They were quiet now, Ben trying to place that expression—*Tell your story walking, Mister*—Roxanne keeping to the right-hand lane on the busy thoroughfare. The radio was tuned to a pop station at a discreet volume, and on a few of the songs Roxanne hummed along, the sound pitch perfect and really quite pleasant.

Now Ben said, "So where are we going for breakfast?"

"My place. I'm cooking."

"Oh, my. You can cook?"

She gave him a playful swat. "Of course I can *cook*."

"What, like those little oatmeal packets? Add water and pop 'em in the microwave?"

"Uh-*uh*. I'm talking about good, old-fashioned cholesterol here, Doctor Hunter. Thickly-sliced back bacon with those globs of yellow fat around the edges. Eggs over-ugly cooked in bacon grease. Home fries oozing butter. All the essential food groups."

"Yum. Can't wait."

"And don't worry, I know CPR."

Ben said, "You'd better," and turned to face her. "So tell me, Roxie. Who is it you want me to meet?"

Roxanne only smiled.

* * *

She was sitting in a wicker rocker on the front porch, reading a paperback novel. A thick one, Ben noticed as they pulled into the driveway, the pages yellowed with age and loving hands. She wore glasses with polarized lenses that hid her eyes, and she didn't look up when the car pulled into the driveway. Her hair was long and snow-white, gathered in a bun on the crown of her head. A knitted shawl covered her shoulders against the morning chill, and she was rocking, a slow, soothing rhythm, one bent finger pulling her gaze across the pages of her book.

When Roxanne killed the engine, Ben said, "Looks like she's really into that novel. That or she's stone-deaf and didn't hear us drive up."

Roxanne chuckled. "Gram says she can hear a mosquito fart at twenty paces. And considering the number of times she's caught me red-handed trying to sneak in after curfew, I'm inclined to agree with her."

"What's that she's reading?"

"*Fellowship of the Ring*. She's had that copy since her teens. She must've read it a dozen times. The rest of the trilogy, too. She can quote it chapter and verse."

Ben thought, *Tolkien*, a tenuous connection lurking just out of reach. *Tell your story walking, Mister.*

Opening the car door now, Roxanne said, "Ready to meet her?"

Ben said, "Sure," and got out of the car.

They were partway up the steps when the connection popped like a road flare in his mind. And even before the woman in the rocker slid the glasses down on her nose and fixed him with those cornflower eyes, he knew who she was.

And in a heartbeat, it all made sense.

He said, "Hello, Melanie."

It took her a moment longer, craning now to squint at him with the sun at his back, and he knew Roxanne hadn't told her who was coming for breakfast.

In the breathless silence that followed, as this exquisitely aged version of the girl he'd loved so long ago made the same connection, Ben felt his heart bolt like the startled squirrel he'd seen with Roxanne that first day by the solar array. Felt the same delicious apprehension he'd experienced sixty years ago on the night of the Sadie Hawkins dance, when he rang the doorbell on a porch just a few blocks from here and the girl who'd stolen his heart with a glance appeared in the doorway, flashing a smile that undid him.

Now Melanie's eyes widened, and she gave him a tentative version of that smile, some of the sparkle gone from it now, faded by the passage of time. She said, "Benjamin Hunter," and rose with an ease that both pleased and surprised him.

Bugging her eyes, Roxanne mouthed the word *Benjamin?* and stifled a giggle. Her grandmother noticed and shot her a scolding glance. Then she opened her arms, saying, "Come here, *Ben*, and give this old broad a hug."

Ben stepped into an embrace that felt like home. After a moment, he said, "She didn't tell you it was me, did she," and gave Roxanne a little stink-eye of his own.

Roxanne was standing behind Gram now, a sappy grin on her face, and when Gram said, "Is she still here?" Roxanne opened the door and hustled inside.

Laughing, she said, "I'm going to make breakfast now," and swung the door shut.

Backing out of the embrace, Melanie said, "My, God, Ben, it's good to see you. How long has it been?"

"Far too long," Ben said, laughing when the curtain twitched and Roxanne's expectant face appeared in the gap. Melanie saw him looking and turned, saying, "That little…" But Roxanne was already gone.

Melanie laughed now too, the unbridled sound lofting him back across an eroded landscape of time. She said, "That child," in mock exasperation, then sat in the rocker, inviting Ben to do the same in the matching chair. For a moment he pictured her husband seated there, then he sat too, legs threatening to fail him in the excitement of this unexpected reunion.

He said, "She's a wonderful girl, your granddaughter."

"She certainly is. And she thinks the world of you, Ben. Since her grandfather passed, you've helped fill a very big hole in her life." She patted his hand. "She's told me a lot about you. Everything but your name. She calls you 'The Doc'."

"Said a lot about me, huh? Some of it good, I hope."

Melanie winked. "A little under half."

"Better than I expected." He pointed at the book in her lap. "Still a Tolkien fan, I see."

"I learn something new every time I read him. Didn't I give you the trilogy for your birthday one time?"

"Christmas. Nineteen-seventy. I still have it."

"But did you *read* it?"

Ben gave her a guilty shrug, saying, "I've never had much time for fiction," and Melanie's warm smile faltered. She said, "Or anything else," and he knew he'd touched a nerve.

"Mel, I—"

"No, Ben, I'm sorry. That was unfair. There's been a lot of water under the bridge since those days. We were young and our paths just…diverged. It happens." She stood now and took his hand, helping him to his feet. "Come on," she said, "I smell bacon frying."

* * *

Melanie enjoyed having a man at the table again, and she loved seeing Roxanne so happy, the two of them constantly joking. She'd spent a lot of time worrying about Roxanne when she was growing up, fearful the child was getting shortchanged being raised by her grandparents instead of her parents. And you could *see* the effects the age difference had had on her: in the conservative, almost prim way she dressed; in the sometimes dated way she spoke; and even more so in her values. Not that there was anything wrong with the way she'd turned out. Quite the opposite. Roxanne had a sharp, inquisitive mind, and had always managed to make the best of both worlds, excelling at the academia *and* breaking hearts with her drop-dead-gorgeous good looks. If there was a problem at all, it was that Roxanne had trouble identifying with her peers, particularly the girls: the sullen, entitled, texting, media-zombified girls that drifted in and out of her life like painted ghosts. As a consequence, she ended up befriending people much older than herself. *Except for Russ*, Melanie thought. *I do like Russ.* Her upbringing had even affected her choice of employment. When she'd come home with the news she'd be spending her year off working at the Geriatric Center, it had come as little surprise to Melanie. And she was constantly hearing from friends who were residents there now about how wonderful her granddaughter was. She couldn't be more proud.

As for Ben—Mel watching him across the table now, the man doing a passable impersonation of Porky Pig and tipping Roxanne into gales of laughter—she could still feel the unexpected pleasure seeing him again had sparked in her, and the attendant upwelling of conflicting emotions. On the one hand, it was great reuniting with someone who'd occupied such a significant part of her youth—they'd been virgins together, for God's sake. But on the other, seeing him again had uncapped a well of heartache and regret she'd sealed shut decades ago—and it had done so in a nanosecond. She'd hugged him, yes, mostly for Roxanne's benefit. But what she'd really wanted was to kiss him the way she had all those years ago—deeply, passionately—lose herself in the glorious tenderness of it. And then punch him in the face.

Watching him now, a part of her felt these were awfully racy thoughts for an old woman to be having. But in truth, only her body had aged. The rest of her—the *her* of her—was just as wanton and alive as that long-ago girl had been. Yet somehow, those parts had lapsed into dormancy, stirred at intervals by a silly romantic comedy, maybe, or the kind of dream from which one awakens moist in places long neglected…but for the most part forgotten.

Her relationship with her husband had been different. Theirs had been more of an intimate companionship, a mutual coming-together born of affection and common goals. He had wanted children, but a severe case of endometriosis after her first pregnancy had left her barren. Years later, after losing her only child to cancer, she'd been secretly relieved she hadn't been able to have more kids. Having more would've meant she might have lost them too, and that was something she couldn't bear. Not ever again.

The one great blessing from all of it was Roxanne.

* * *

The morning passed quickly, almost noon before Roxanne suggested the 'old folks' head back to the porch while she cleaned up the kitchen.

But Melanie decided she'd had enough for one day, and said she felt a migraine coming on. She told Ben how much she'd enjoyed seeing him again, then made her way up to her room.

In curtained sunlight, she dug a stack of old diaries out of the closet and sat in a rocker by the window, opening the volume labeled *The Benjamin Years* in the cursive script of her youth. She laughed when she saw the tiny red hearts she'd dotted her *i*'s with in those days. She'd been sixteen that first year, and Ben had come into her life with all the force of a feather on a dead calm day. God, but he'd been *shy*.

She read until she heard them leave—at breakfast Roxanne had said she was driving Ben to a doctor's appointment this afternoon, but hadn't elaborated—then put the diaries aside. She went into the ensuite to scrub away the tears that had dried to silvery crusts on her face, the ones from her laughter mixed indistinguishably with those born of sadness, then decided to lie down after all. There was an ache behind her eyes now, not a full-blown migraine, but bad enough to knock the stuffing out of her for a while.

She knew she'd be seeing Ben Hunter again. She'd seen it not only in his eyes, but also in Roxanne's. And while she was okay with that, she'd already drawn a line in the sand. If he wanted to be friends, that was fine; he was important to Roxanne, and her happiness meant more to Melanie than her own. But it could never be more than that. Most of her reasons were etched in the time-faded diary of a teenage girl.

But her main reason was much darker.

There was something wrong with Ben Hunter. And she was almost certain she knew what it was.

* * *

Roxanne said, "What are you thinking about?"

They were sitting in the ER lounge, waiting for Ben's appointment with Dr. Skeen. On the drive over, they'd stopped by Ben's apartment to pick up one of the blister packs his colleague Jake had sent. Quinn had left the parcel on the kitchen counter with a note that said, *Good luck, you crusty old bastard!*

It was ten minutes to three.

Ben said, "I was thinking about you, actually."

"Really?"

He nodded. "You and a term my grandfather used to use."

"What was that?"

"Greasy."

Roxanne poked him in the ribs. "Is that some kind of slur on my cooking?"

"Not at all. Breakfast was delicious."

"You sound surprised."

He said, "I suppose I am," and she poked him again.

"So what made you think of it?"

"Think of what?"

"Greasy."

"If a person did something Grump thought was sneaky, he'd say it was 'greasy'. We called him Grump because he always looked angry, but he was the sweetest man I ever—"

Roxanne gave him an exasperated look. "So what did *I* do that was *greasy*?"

"Not telling your grandmother who was coming for breakfast." He laughed at her *Who me?* expression, saying, "And don't give me that innocent look. You *knew* about her and I, didn't you."

Roxanne only smiled.

Ben was about to ask how she'd found out when the obvious answer struck him. He said, "Your grandmother told you, right? You *did* tell her my name and she put it together from there. And she just faked being surprised to see me."

"No, actually. Until the past little while, I barely mentioned you at all. Just the once, I think, right after we met, and all I told her then was I'd met a retired doctor who helped me decide about Gramps." She directed her gaze at the floor now, cheeks flushing pink. "You and I got close so fast, Ben, I didn't want her thinking, you know, I'd replaced Gramps with someone else."

"I understand. I really do. But that doesn't answer my question. How did you find out about your grandmother and I?"

Roxanne met his gaze now and he could see the mischief in her eyes.

She said, "Ely."

"Ely? But how...?"

"She found a portrait of you and Gram she'd done when you were teenagers. A beautiful pastel." Grinning, she said, "You were quite the hunk, *Ben*jamin Hunter. All dark and brooding."

Laughing, Ben said, "Remind me to show you the slides from my GQ photo shoot," and a nurse called his name.

* * *

The nurse led them to a treatment room at the end of a cluttered corridor, elderly patients in open stalls watching hollow-eyed as the trio filed past in slow procession. Dr. Skeen was already in the room, arranging ampoules on a trolley table. Ben introduced Roxanne to the doctor and asked if she could remain in the room. Skeen said it was fine, but told Roxanne if Ben showed even the slightest sign of an allergic reaction, she'd have to return to the lounge.

Roxanne sat in a chair while the doctor helped Ben into a sitting position on a paper-sheeted examining table.

Now Skeen said, "So let's see this stuff."

Ben handed over the six-capsule blister pack he'd taken from the box of fifty Jake had sent.

Holding it up for Roxanne to see, Skeen said, "Doesn't look like much, does it, Roxanne. But your wise old friend here has helped improve the lives of millions of dementia sufferers with this little miracle." He gave the pack a shake. It sounded like a maraca. "And now it's his turn to benefit."

Flushed, embarrassed by the praise and Roxanne's admiring gaze, Ben said, "Well, best not get ahead of ourselves, Trevor. The original formulation almost put me in the ground."

Dr. Skeen returned the blister pack to Ben, saying, "When I spoke with your colleague, he seemed confident you'd be fine." He indicated the trolley table. "And we're ready for anything here."

Nodding, Ben popped one of the soft-gels into his palm. Skeen filled a paper cup with tap water and handed it to him. Ben said, "Moment of truth," tossed the blue-and-white capsule into his mouth and chased it with a slug of water. He returned the cup to Skeen and lay back on the examining table, the paper sheet crinkling under his weight.

Roxanne pulled her chair closer and held Ben's hand.

Skeen said, "About how long did it take you to react last time?"

Ben said, "I don't remember much about that day, but I was told I was seizing in under a minute."

The doctor glanced at his watch. "Okay. Let's see what happens."

The room lapsed into an anticipatory silence.

Ben counted to a hundred in his head—then ran his tongue out and began to shimmy and shake like a man possessed. Roxanne sprang to her feet saying, "Doctor *Skeen*," and Ben watched the man roll his eyes and smirk. Unable to help himself, Ben laughed.

Jerking her hand away, Roxanne said, "That wasn't *funny*."

But Skeen was laughing now too, dabbing his eyes with a square of gauze. He said, "It *was* pretty funny," and Roxanne broke into a fit of nervous giggles.

When things settled—Ben up on his elbow now, looking healthy as a horse—Skeen checked his watch again. "Three minutes down, twenty-seven to go." He opened the examining room door. "I'll be right down the hall. And Roxanne, if your friend starts convulsing again, just douse him with a cup of cold water."

Roxanne said, "With pleasure," and gave Ben's neck a goosey pinch.

* * *

Ben suffered no more reaction to the capsule than a wet burp that tasted like bacon. Skeen gave him a clean bill of health, Roxanne walked him back to his apartment, and Ben called Jake to give him the good news. Ben agreed to keep a written diary of his progress and signed off, as exhilarated as he'd ever been.

He watched TV for a while, but couldn't concentrate. Seeing Melanie again had filled his heart with gladness and hope. She was single now, mature enough to have mourned her husband months ago. And when she hugged him on the porch, there'd been a moment so familiar and smoldering hot, he'd been sure she was going to kiss him full on the mouth—but a few seconds later, when she backed out of the embrace, he'd been equally certain she was going to punch him in the face.

Mixed feelings. The best kind. He smiled and headed for the kitchen.

It was almost time for his second dose of the isomer.

* * *

Ben had just stripped down to his boxers that night when a faint knock came at the apartment door. It was Ray, fishbelly white, rail-thin in his wash-faded T-shirt and jeans. Breathing hard, he said, "Hey, buddy. It's time."

183

NINE

BEN WAS SHOCKED BY his friend's appearance. He'd seen end-stage disease many times in his medical practice, but it was a much tougher spectacle to witness in someone you loved. Ray's body was cannibalizing itself, and Ben could see he was on his last legs.

He said, "Okay, yes. If you're ready, I'm ready," and started out the door.

Ray managed a feeble laugh. "This is what you're wearing to my big send off?"

Ben glanced in the mirror, seeing nothing on his bony frame but blue-check boxers. He said, "Jesus Christ, I'm sorry, man. Come in." Ray stepped in and Ben said, "Grab a beer if you like. Take the edge off."

"Thanks, but I just came from Wilder's place. Quinn was there and we lit a farewell joint. Acapulco Red. Very mellow." He chuckled. "I had no idea Quinn was such a pussy."

"Got a bit weepy, did he?"

"Like a little girl."

Ben said, "That's my job," and padded into the bedroom, hoping Ray couldn't hear his shattered sobs.

* * *

Breaking the oppressive silence in the elevator, Ben said, "Turns out Roxanne's grandmother is Melanie Anderson." He hadn't meant to bring it up, judging this a poor time to be talking about his own life, but it just popped out. "Remember her?"

"*Remember* her," Ray said, bugging those blue eyes. "How could I forget? You pissed and moaned about that girl for a decade after she dumped you. That year we shared the apartment on Lisgar Street? I wanted to hold a pillow over your face while you slept. Melanie this, Melanie that." He grinned through the pain he was clearly suffering. "She still married?"

"Her husband passed."

"So you gonna try and hook up with her again?"

Since seeing Melanie, he'd been thinking of little else. But he said, "A bit late for that, don't you think?"

Quick as a Ninja, Ray punched him on the shoulder, the blow surprisingly sharp given the man's condition. Ben shot him a dirty look, but he knew what the jab was for. Since grade school it had signified BULLSHIT, and when fairly administered, never provoked retaliation.

Ray said, "Stings, don't it," and Ben nodded.

The elevator stopped and the men got out, bearing left now through the lobby to the glass-covered walkway leading to the Euthanasia Foundation.

As they walked, Ray said, "I know you're the doctor and I'm just the paint-and-wallpaper guy, but for once in your life you need to listen to me, because I only have time to say this once. It is *never* too late to bring love into your life. I learned that firsthand with my Bella. And I know you're capable of it, because I know you love me."

Ray caught him by the arm and they stopped to face each other in the walkway, the night sky above a basin of stars, a thin rind of moon snagged in the treetops out there.

Releasing Ben's arm, Ray said, "The six years I had with Bella, if that had been the sum total of my time on Earth, it would've been enough. I mean that. So if your heart soared when you saw her, if you've been thinking of nothing else since that moment—" Ray slammed him on the shoulder again, harder this time. "—then go for it, you dim bulb. Because if you don't, I'll come back and haunt your ass for the rest of your miserable life. Understood?"

"Yeah, I get it. And thanks, man. Thanks a lot."

Ray said, "Grow some balls," and they started walking again.

Rubbing his shoulder, Ben said, "That's gonna leave a mark."

"It was supposed to. Let it serve as a reminder."

And in the wistful, exhilarating, and often confusing weeks ahead, it did exactly that.

* * *

Ray said, "So what's the plan?"

"There *is* no plan. We play it by ear."

"What if we get stopped by security?"

"You kick him in the balls and I shoot him with his own gun."

"Come on, man."

"You're just going to have to trust me, okay? There'll likely be a guard at the main entrance, but if it's the guy I think it'll be, there's a reasonable chance he'll let me take you on a tour of the place. I looked after his mother years ago and he still thinks he owes me."

"A tour. At this hour?"

"I said a *rea*sonable chance."

"And if it's not him?"

"There's more than one way to skin a cat. Just stay behind me and be quiet."

"Yes, Dad."

The walkway opened onto the ground floor of the Foundation in a broad hallway encircling the atrium. The men peeked around the doorway to see a security guard seated at a table by the main entrance, a portly guy hunched over a paperback in the glow of a pot light.

Keeping his voice down, Ray said, "That your guy?"

Ben shook his head. "Never seen him before. Let's head back."

They backtracked to the service entrance of the admin building, down a set of metal steps to a delivery bay that gave onto an adjacent parking lot. Moving briskly in the night air, Ben said, "This way," and turned left onto a lockstone path lit at intervals by solar lamps.

Trailing him, Ray said, "Slow down, man. You're gonna give me a heart attack before we can get this done."

But Ben didn't hear him. He was functioning solely on hindbrain now, the front of his mind filled with white noise.

The path led to the rear of the Foundation, bringing the men around the curving hip of the building to a staff entrance with a dimly-lit keypad. Ben bent to squint at the numbers, fingers trembling as he punched in a four-digit code he hadn't used in a decade. The keypad beeped once, clicked—and a red LED lit up, the digital display flashing the word *ERROR* in pale blue characters.

Ben said, *"Shit,"* and tried again, more carefully this time, Ray hovering behind him now, the man's labored breathing the only sound.

This time when the damn thing beeped, the green LED flashed and Ben heard the locking mechanism release.

He opened the door and pulled Ray inside, saying, "I *knew* the bastards'd be too lazy to terminate my access code." He pointed at the ceiling. "Keep your head down. Security cameras."

Chuckling, Ray said, "I think we're beyond that mattering much anymore," and Ben chuckled too, his tension abating in the face of this simple truth.

He paused now to embrace his friend—fiercely, passionately, as if in holding onto the man he was holding onto life itself—then released him, saying, "Fuck 'em if they can't take a joke."

"Yeah," Ray said, "Fuck 'em."

And as if they'd rehearsed it, both men faced the camera and flipped it the bird, twirling in tight little hip-thrusting circles before taking off down the hall.

* * *

Wilf Birmingham, head of security for the nightshift, turned from the card game on his iPad to the bank of monitors, amused to see two old dudes staring up at him on camera 83, flipping him the bird in a silent pirouette.

Then he recognized Dr. Hunter.

"What the...?"

He checked his watch—after curfew—then radioed Ike Booth, his man at the desk in the Euthanasia Foundation, telling him to get his ass around to the parking lot entrance.

* * *

Ben said, "We can't stop them from getting into the building, but we *can* keep them out of the suite. For a while, at least."

They entered the atrium with its domed ceiling made of glass. The building itself was only three stories, but the effect of the dome was breathtaking, and Ray paused to gaze up at it. The crescent moon hung dead center up there now, and Ray appeared almost spectral in its brilliance.

In the face of what they were about to do, Ben had to look away. He said, "Ray, come on," and headed for the curving staircase. "The suites are on the second floor."

The men hurried up the marble staircase now, winded from their exertions and the unremitting tension, footfalls echoing in the deceptive opulence of the place. Right or wrong, this was a house of death, and for the first time since he'd championed its creation, Ben shuddered within its walls.

As they made the landing, Ben heard a door open down below followed by a raised voice: *"Show yourselves, gentlemen!"*

Breathless, he bent to the keypad at the first suite they came to and punched in the code. Seizing Ray's arm, he said, "In here," and pushed the door open, guiding his friend inside.

Now he bolted the door and a series of baseboard lights came on, casting a pale glow. Ben strode to the technician's console, picked up a cannonball-size sculpture in bronze of a grinning Buddha, and used it to smash the keypad by the door. "Won't keep them out forever," he said, "but it'll sure as hell slow them down."

Replacing the Buddha on the console, Ben said, "Privacy laws prohibit cameras up here, so it'll take them a while to sort out which suite we're in, and another good while to get inside."

Nodding, Ray slung an arm around Ben's shoulders and they stood in silence for a beat, gazing through a glass panel into the unlit theater, the thin wash of light from the control room picking up random gleams in there.

Now Ben said, "Are you absolutely certain you want to do this?"

"As sure as I've ever been about anything," Ray said. "I know you don't believe in God or Heaven or any of the other lofty concepts they terrified us with in Catholic school. And while I'm with you on most of it, I do believe in a higher power, some balancing force holding it all together. The way I see it, we're all made of the same stuff. And for every one of us, there comes a time when we have to go back into the soup. Think of it as recycling. I've had my run. In a long life, I've had one great friend—quit grinning, you jackass; you thought I meant you?" Ben laughed. "And one great woman. And now I'm ready to tip this old carcass into the cosmic blue bin. But I want to do it on my own terms, with dignity—without any more pain—and with my best friend at the helm. Is that too much to ask?"

With tears in his eyes, Ben agreed it wasn't. He said, "Okay, buddy," and opened the theater door. "Strange as it may sound under the circumstances, I think you're going to enjoy this."

* * *

The euthanasia theater—circular, like the atrium— was surprisingly spacious, and Ray felt only the slightest apprehension as Ben locked the door and a series of muted baseboard lights came on, as they had in the outer chamber. A comfy-looking bed stood in the center of the room, and the bare walls were a soothing sand color. Not much else in here besides that, just an adjustable IV pole suspended from the ceiling, and a single tan wingchair matching the walls.

Before Ben could tell him to, Ray lay on the bed, the memory-foam molding to his every contour. Settling in, he said, "God damn. If I could afford a mattress like this, I bet I could sleep at night." He batted his eyes at Ben now, a clown to the end. "Wanna climb aboard for one last romp?"

Ben said, "You couldn't handle it," and they laughed like the boys they'd once been.

After a quiet moment, Ben said, "Remember the film *Soylent Green*?"

"Charlton Heston, right? '*Soylent Green is* people!'"

Ben said, "Exactly," and typed something on a recessed keyboard. "Well, I stole the idea for the suites from that movie. Check this out."

At first, nothing happened. Then the curving walls began to glow a pale, shimmering blue, like shallow seawater under a tropical sun.

Ben said, "Remember Heston's roommate? The old guy, Sol Roth?"

"Yeah, played by Edward G. Robinson."

"Right. Remember the scene—?"

"*Right.* Everyone lining up at that huge euthanasia facility to end their lives of poverty and starvation. And Heston's character, Detective..."

"Thorn."

"Yeah, Detective Thorn, catches up to the old man before he goes off to sleep, and the room is like an iMax theater."

And even as he said it the walls came alive, an almost subaural bass rumble resolving into the chant of a crowd...hippies, thousands of them, shirtless and tan, dancing artlessly with flowers in their hair, eyelids heavy with peace and illicit substances. Ray said, "Woodstock," just as the wraparound scene cut to the moonlit stage and a stoned Alvin Lee said into the mic, "Here's a little thing called "I'm Goin' Home" by Helicopter," and broke into one of Ray's favorite performances.

"Jesus," Ray said, the experience immersive, like being there, only without the mud, mosquitos, and unwashed neighbors. "Jesus."

Ben said, "Dig it, my friend," and stuck an IV needle into the back of Ray's hand. "I'll be right back."

* * *

Ike Booth radioed his boss from the second floor of the Euthanasia Foundation—what the residents called Terminal House or sometimes the Euth Club—and told him there was no sign of the two old men. Out of breath, he said, "I've been all through the building. It's like they disappeared."

Ike hated this friggin' place; it gave him the creeps. His mother always said he had a touch of the shine, and since they'd saddled him with this sector on permanent nights, he'd come to believe her. There were ghosts in here, lots of them, lurking just out of sight.

His boss said, "Well, they're in there somewhere, Booth, because I haven't seen them come out. I want you to open every door, look in every closet, under every desk and in every shitter until you *find* them. You hear? Because if I have to call the CEO about this—at this time of night—there's going to be hell to pay and it's going to come out of your hide."

Ike said, "Copy that," and signed off. There were five suites up here, and he started with the one closest to him—*The Trudeau Suite*—thinking, *Why in the name of Christ would anyone want one of these Nazi extermination chambers named after them?*

He punched in the code with a shaky finger, wishing he'd called in sick like he'd almost done, the chili his wife had served him for dinner bloating him up like a damn beach ball.

He entered the suite and those muted lights came on, raising shadows that seemed to caper. He knew the effect was supposed to be calming, but it gave him the willies.

He said, "Anyone in here?" and groped around for the main light switch.

* * *

Ben pecked at the keyboard in the control room, calculating an infusion rate for the medications he'd be delivering to Ray intravenously. The potent pharmaceuticals would arrive in a prescribed sequence, the intent being to provide the men with adequate time to say goodbye; then, gradually, to ease Ray into a peaceful slumber from which he would never awaken. It was a tried-and-true formula Ben had created over a decade ago, and in the interim no one had seen any reason to change it.

The first infusion, which Ben commenced now, was a combination of meds used routinely in anesthesia: Propofol—nicknamed Milk of Amnesia due to its milky color and hypnotic qualities—and Remifentanil, a synthetic narcotic so potent that in the anesthetic setting, it had to be administered in fractions of a milligram per kilogram. Over the next fifteen minutes, the infusion rate would gradually increase, amplifying the effect from a barely perceptible sense of serenity to the best and cleanest high Ray had ever experienced. From there, over the course of the subsequent few minutes, his eyelids would grow heavy and he'd drift off to sleep. At this point, based on physiological signals detected by sensors in the mattress, a powerful paralyzing agent would be added to the mix, and within seconds Ray would stop breathing. The infusion would continue until the occurrence of clinical death, a state again determined by embedded sensors.

That was the science of the thing.

Now, for the first time as a friend instead of a clinician, Ben had to confront the finality of it head on.

He sat in the wingchair next to the bed and took Ray's hand, Ten Years After still ripping it up at Woodstock.

* * *

Ray started at his friend's touch, already aware of the drugs coursing through him in a gentle tide. Watching Lee play that big red Gibson, he felt a pang of regret that he and Ben hadn't made it to the iconic gathering that was Woodstock. They'd intended to, had even mapped out the trip from Ottawa to Max Yasgur's six-hundred-acre dairy farm in the Catskills. But when they asked their boss for the time off, the man had told them sure, go ahead—but when you get back, you'll be unemployed. Deciding to catch the next big festival that came along, they gave up Woodstock for their buck-thirty-an-hour jobs slinging pizza dough. *Jesus.* Who knew? Hendrix. Cocker. Santana. Goddamn Ten Years After. Nothing remotely like it had happened again. Three days of peace and music.

Now the scene changed to Hendrix jamming the national anthem.

Watching Jimi do his thing, Ray said, "You know what'd be a great video for in here?"

"What?"

"Queen doing, "Another One Bites the Dust"."

Ben said, "You asshole," and Ray managed a weak chuckle.

Squeezing Ben's hand now, Ray said, "There's no going back, is there, amigo."

"No, there sure as hell isn't. And I'm not sure I would if I could."

"Probably just fuck it up all over again."

"Guaranteed."

Ray glanced at Hendrix, the soulful wail of the man's guitar making his skin tingle. Now his eyes were on Ben, watching with curiosity as he slid a homemade DVD into the video console in the bedframe.

"What's that?" he said, stoned now, his speech beginning to slur.

Ben smiled. "Bootleg. The video quality sucks, but trust me, you're gonna love it. After we talked about what was the coolest thing we'd ever done together, I remembered having this. I got it from a roadie maybe twenty-five years ago, then forgot I had it."

Fading fast now, Ray said, "Roadie for who?" just as Robert Plant appeared on the screen in grainy black-

and-white, John Bonham thundering behind him, the band exploding into "Communication Breakdown."

"Zeppelin," Ray said. "God, look how young they are there." Now his head came off the pillow. "Wait. Is that...?"

Ben laughed. "Damn straight it is. Civic Center, April seventeenth, nineteen-seventy."

"Holy *shit*. That was the night *we* saw them. How did you get this?"

"Roadie, like I said. I got sentimental one night and started cruising the Internet for bootlegs, thinking how cool it'd be to hear that concert again. But this guy did us one better and videotaped it on thirty-five millimeter. Parts of it, anyway. That's how he got these great side-stage shots. Sucker was right *there*."

"Holy *shit*."

"You said that already."

"Well, it needed to be said again. The tickets were four bucks, remember?"

"Four-fifty at the door." Pointing at the screen now, Ben said, "All right, you need to pay attention—right here."

"*Holy*— Was that...?"

Ben hit the rewind button and Plant spun the mic at exaggerated speed, the shot cutting to the front of the stage now and all those excited young faces in the pit, long hair flailing. Now the video paused, obscuring the image—then flickered ahead in slow motion, closing on two shaggy heads partially hidden by the monitors, faceless at first, then rising up in unison in a transported bounce, shining faces visible now, at once familiar and long-forgotten.

Ray said, "Jesus Christ…that's *us*."

Then he closed his eyes.

* * *

Ben kissed his friend on the forehead, startled now by a ferocious banging at the door and an urgent voice over the PA system.

"Hunter, what the *hell* are you up to in there?"

It was Hicks, the CEO.

Ben felt Ray's neck for a pulse and found none. He said, "I love you, man," and unlocked the theater door.

TEN

SHADOWED BY A SURLY security guard, Hicks led Ben to his office on the main floor of the admin building, tugging him along by the sleeve until Ben jerked his arm away. Without a word, Hicks dismissed the guard and opened the office door, indicating the chair in front of his desk as the lights came on. "Sit," he said, and Ben did, an acid mix of grief and dread churning in his guts.

Shrugging out of his overcoat now, Hicks shook his head, his corned-beef complexion darkening to an unhealthy plum color. Watching him, Ben entertained the slender hope the son of a bitch would have a coronary right here in his richly-appointed inner sanctum.

No such luck.

Hicks strode into the space behind his desk, draped his coat over the back of his antique-leather executive chair, and lobbed the key to his two-hundred-thousand-dollar Mercedes SLR onto the desk. Adjusting his suit coat, he eased himself into the chair with practiced elegance, steepling his fingers under his chin, looking directly at Ben now. Angering Hicks further, Ben held the man's laser gaze without flinching, thinking, *If looks could kill, I'd already be dead.*

Hicks said, "Do you have any idea the kind of trouble you're in?"

Ben said nothing.

"You'd better talk to me, old man, because I am *this* close to picking up the phone and calling the RCMP. That was murder you committed in there, and I'm telling you right now, the Mounties aren't going to give a rarefied *fuck* who you are or who you *think* you are, you're going to spend the rest of your miserable life in prison."

Ben thought, *Fuck 'em if they can't take a joke,* and grinned, knowing exactly how he was going to handle this. He said, "So call them."

Hicks was on his feet now. *"You think this is a* joke?*"*

Ben reached across the desk and slid the phone toward Hicks, using his free hand to palm the man's car key.

Turning that nasty plum color again, Hicks picked up the receiver. "You think I'm screwing around?" He switched the unit to speaker, dialed 411 and waited, saying, "Ottawa," and "No," to the computerized prompts. When he said, "Royal Canadian Mounted Police," Ben said, "But you might want to reconsider."

Hicks glared at him, apparently determined to continue—but something in Ben's calm gaze backed him down. He cut the connection but held onto the receiver, saying, "And why would I do that?"

"You know goddamn well why. Now sit."

Hicks cradled the receiver and sat, confirming a suspicion Ben had harbored for years. He thought, *Bastard, I own you now.*

Ben said, "Do you recall a fellow by the name of Samuel Cleary?" and watched Hicks's mouth drop open like the hatch on a garbage chute. "Old classmate of yours, if I'm not mistaken. Gambling problem?"

"I have no idea who you're talking about."

"Oh, I believe you do. I noticed it about a year after you took over for Robb Flemming as CEO. Decent man, Robb. Shame about his heart. It struck me as extravagant, you know, nine hundred thousand over a ten-month period for 'physician recruitment'. The checks made out to Cleary and Associates. I expect a quick accounts-payable audit would clear this up. How much did old Sammy-boy kick back to you, Clifford? Fifty percent? Seventy five?"

Hicks started to object, then slumped in his chair. "Why didn't you expose me back then?"

"Because I wasn't certain. And we were facing enough controversy over the Euthanasia Foundation. I was afraid a scandal like this would bring it all crashing down."

"And now?"

"An even trade. You clean this up, I take it to the grave. Assuming you're not still embezzling."

Hicks shook his head. "Sam's dead now. Brain tumor. The prick threatened my family, Hunter. I had no choice."

Rising, Ben said, "There's always a choice, Clifford. Always."

Hicks said, "Easy for you to say," and got to his feet. "All right, you win. Now get the hell out of my office so I can sort this out and maybe get home before sunrise. And if you *ever* pull a stunt like this again—"

"It'll never happen again," Ben said, bone-tired now, content to let the prick have the last word. Turning to leave, he said, "He was my best friend, Clifford, and he begged me to do it. And don't worry, I had him fill out the proper forms. I left the box for the technician's name blank. All you've gotta do is fill it in. And please, see that his remains are treated with respect. He was a better man than both of us." He made his way to the door now, droop-shouldered with sadness and fatigue. Before leaving, he said, "And Cliff?"

"What?"

"In the future, try not to be such an asshole."

* * *

Still fully dressed, Ben lay in bed and closed his eyes, as exhausted as he'd ever been. He thought of Ray, the way his eyes had lit up when he saw their teenage selves grooving to the great Led Zeppelin, thinking the timing couldn't have been better.

And in a fast-forward reel of comic vignettes, he relived some of the sidesplitting stunts Ray had pulled in those days: coming out of a gas station bathroom with the leading edge of a roll of toilet paper stuffed down the back of his jeans, the roll unspooling through the open doorway, Ray feigning embarrassment when people began to notice but continuing to walk just the same; belting out a prolonged shriek of horror in another bathroom, this one in a respectable restaurant, while he, Ben, sat among the capacity crowd, everyone freezing at the horrific cry, Ray waltzing out a few seconds later as if nothing had happened; offering to buy snacks for a party of six that included himself, his wife Angie, Ben and his date, and another couple at the premiere of the movie M*A*S*H in 1972, returning a few minutes later with a cardboard tray crammed with popcorn and pop, pretending he'd forgotten where they were sitting, Angie hissing at him now—*Ray, Ray!*—Ray scanning the theater but continuing to walk—*RAY!*—then doing a pratfall in mock alarm, the vats of popcorn and pop exploding down the aisle, the sold-out crowd roaring laughter while Angie sat in furious silence, face burning hellfire-red in the dark...

So many good times. It had been like having his own standup comic for a best friend, every last one of those gags and countless others intended solely for his amusement. What a wonderful guy. He would miss Ray mightily. But once he'd gotten a clear sense of the man's suffering and how long it had been going on, he had to concede there was no other option.

Following these precious reflections, Ben lapsed into a kind of exhausted semitrance, half-aware of his resting self and half-invested in something that might have been a memory, the fringes of a dream, or a fatigued variant of dementia. In it, he was about to have sex for the first time—or some frenzied, adolescent version of it—fumbling with his belt, shoulder aching from leaning on the bottom mattress of the creaky bunk bed he shared with his brother, the girl beneath him scrambling to get her jeans off, both of them breathing hard, giddy with anticipation, ditching school today to get the deed done. Now he fumbled his way inside her and it was warm and wet and enveloping, and he felt himself already on the verge, and now she swept the hair out of her face and it was—

Roxanne

Ben sat bolt upright, clothes stuck to his baking skin, the first real erection he'd had in years straining against the fabric of his trousers.

Now the room was spinning and he was on his feet, lurching from handhold to handhold to slump over the toilet, the contents of his stomach geysering up his throat.

He hunched there a while, waiting to see if there was more. But he'd wrung himself out, and now he sat on the toilet seat, feeling like the worst kind of deviant, wondering what on earth was wrong with him.

Once the room agreed to stand still, he flushed the toilet and stoppered the sink, cranking the cold tap to full blast. Waiting for the bowl to fill, he glanced in the mirror, seeing a stooped old man gaping back at him, really *seeing* him, a seventy-eight-year-old man having erotic fantasies about a girl he'd come to love—but God, not *that* way. If this was what dementia was going to be like for him, his mind serving up horrific shit like this… well, it might just be time to fill out those euthanasia forms for himself.

He shut off the tap, bent to submerge his face and heard a brisk knock at the apartment door, followed by frantic, muffled voices. He checked his watch—twenty past midnight—and wondered if it was Hicks calling his bluff, bringing a couple of cops along to haul him off to jail. But as he made his way to the foyer, he recognized one of the voices—*Quinn*—and thought, *What the hell is it now?*

He opened the apartment door.

* * *

Three hours earlier, Ben's nearest neighbor—an eighty-year-old Russian physicist by the name of Viktor Sokolov—had been hatching an escape plan.

But perhaps 'escape' is too strong a word, Viktor thought now, the fact that he might be in serious trouble beginning to dawn on him. He didn't want to leave the Center for good. Just for the night. He had it all arranged, his appointment at Rubens scheduled for two AM. He'd never been there in person, but he'd been a regular on their website for several months. And in that time, he'd fallen helplessly in love with a twenty-eight-year-old working girl named Lisa, whose statistics were prodigious: three hundred and thirty-six pounds of pale, powdered flesh that took his breath away. He knew the IT guys were going to catch up with him soon enough, cut off his Internet access and ban him from using the computers in the library, probably for life. The Center's rules regarding porn sites were clear and inflexible. But the delight he derived from his sessions with Lisa were worth the risk. *And* the cost.

The thing of it was, he wanted to *be* with her now. Do some of the things she promised in their online chats. Explore the vast mounds and musky valleys he'd glimpsed on the screen. But there was a problem—a humiliating one. About a month ago, his prick had stopped working. No warning. No ceremony. The brute had simply died. True, he'd had a good run with the thing. Until this merciless betrayal, his pecker had always been up before him in the morning, ready for action at the slightest provocation. And in the size department, the gods had been more than generous, his willy already seven inches long when it sprouted its first hair, Viktor a twelve-year-old farmboy at the time. And it hadn't stopped growing until he was nineteen, maxing out at eight inches at ease, ten-and-a-half at full attention, hard enough to deflect bullets. He'd even appeared in a few Russian porn films in his twenties, wearing a black-leather fetish mask and collecting easy money for school, Saint Petersburg Polytechnic, where he'd earned a PhD in experimental physics. In the many years since, he'd buried three wives and pleasured uncountable mistresses. And under different circumstances, he might have allowed his wang a well-earned retirement.

But then there was Lisa. Sweet, bulbous, breathy Lisa, spread out like a fleshy fairground on a bed the size of an aircraft carrier. And here *he* was, a broke-dick Ruski hound dog with a thriving libido and nothing to back it up with. He knew the condition was treatable, all sorts of drugs out there for erectile dysfunction. But Viktor was a proud man, and he didn't want to admit to *any*one, not even a doctor, that the magnificent instrument that had served him so well had finally given up the ghost.

It was a dilemma.

He'd tried all manner of over-the-counter remedies: Panax Ginseng, Rhodalia Rosea, DHEA. He'd even performed acupuncture on himself, using needles he'd pilfered from one of the rehab therapists, his dink bristling like a porcupine before he was done. But nothing had worked.

Until yesterday, when a solution presented itself. On his way down to lunch, he'd spotted an unattended med cart in the hallway, the pharmacy tech a few doors down at the time, lending a hand at a code blue. And there, right on top of the cart, stood a big white bottle of bliss: Tumidol. He'd just seen a commercial about it on the tube, a silver-haired dude on a 747 sneaking off to service his old lady in one of those cramped bathroom stalls, joining the Mile High Club at the ripe old age of seventy-five.

Viktor had pocketed the bottle and kept on walking, pausing en route to the elevators to peek in on the failing resuscitation in apartment 9017, the widow Brunet on the floor in there, looking much the worse for wear. He'd had that little minx on the floor himself, and in the bed, against the fridge, in the shower stall...

So the plan had been simple. Make the appointment at Rubens, take one of the pills (he'd taken three, for courage), slip out of the Center through a rear door he knew had a busted alarm, and stroll across the road to the Tim Horton's, where he'd have a cab waiting. Spend the night with Lisa, *God save me,* grab a cab in the morning and slip back into the Center undetected.

But the bastards had fixed the alarm, and he was caught before he made it halfway across the parking lot. A dark green sedan with a twirling blue light on the dash overtook him, and one of those grim black-shirts hopped out to escort him back inside, the man as mute as a statue, his grip on Viktor's arm letting him know resistance would not only be futile, but quite possibly bad for his health. By the time he got back to his apartment, the pills had kicked in and his johnson had regained its former magnificence. Painfully so.

That had been three hours ago, and the thing was still plank-hard.

* * *

Ben barely had the door open when Quinn barged past him into the foyer, dragging a distressed Viktor Sokolov by the wrist, Wilder bringing up the rear with an amused grin on his face, ambling in like he had all the time in the world.

Shutting the door behind this strange trio, Ben said, "What the hell, guys? It's after midnight."

Quinn regarded him in frank alarm, then looked at Viktor, saying, "Show him," and Viktor dropped his baggy sweatpants around his ankles.

Before he knew what was happening, Ben was staring at a huge, purple, grossly-engorged member, the thing bobbing out of the man's pants like an exit barricade at the gates of Hell.

Ben said, "*Jesus,*" and recoiled a few steps, his stomach threatening to turn again. "What in the name of God…?"

Quinn said, "He OD'ed on boner pills and now he's afraid the damn thing's going to explode. And not in a good way." He leaned in for a closer look. "I'm no doctor, Benji, but I'm inclined to agree with the man."

Viktor only moaned.

Lurking behind them, Wilder stifled a giggle.

Quinn said, "It's not funny, man."

"I'd have to agree with you there," Wilder said. "It's goddamn *hilarious.*"

Quinn said, "Asshole," and turned to Ben. "What are we gonna do?"

Laughing now, Wilder said, "Quinn, you're gonna have to suck him off," and Ben could see the man was high as a kite. Nothing new there.

Concerned, Ben said, "All right, Viktor, listen, you're going to have to take that thing to the ER. You might actually need surgery. Now why don't you pull up your pants and I'll give them a call, let them know we're coming."

Trying to pull up his pants—Quinn stooping to help him now, almost getting that dusky helmet in the eye— Viktor said, "Coming, yes. Wouldn't that help?"

Ben said, "Probably, but I was assuming you already tried that."

Viktor shook his head.

Wilder said, "Quinn, you're already down there," and Quinn sprang to his full height, looking like he might actually take a swing at his grinning friend.

Chuckling, Wilder faded into the kitchen to raid the fridge. Ben saw him grab an entire six-pack of beer off the bottom shelf, lacing those big fingers through the spaces in the plastic yoke, but he was beyond caring.

Knotting the strings on his sweatpants, Viktor eased onto the couch and told the men about his plans for the evening, saying they still had over an hour to get him there. Saying he'd beg if he had to.

Ben was about to tell the man to forget it, they were going straight to the ER. Then he remembered Hicks's car key, still in his hip pocket. He took it out, liking its heft. He said, "What time's your appointment?"

"Two o'clock."

"All right. If we leave now, we should get there with time to spare." He looked at Viktor. "But if an hour with what's her name…"

Viktor said, "Lisa," and licked his lips, as if the word had a pleasing taste.

Smiling, Ben said, "If your session with 'Lisa' doesn't get rid of…" pointing at the bulge in the man's sweat-pants now, "*that*, then our next stop's the emergency department. Agreed?"

"Agreed."

"Okay, gentlemen," Ben said, showing them the car key. "I'm driving."

Wilder left the apartment first, followed by Viktor, the poor guy not moving very fast. Ben started out next, but Quinn caught him by the arm, saying in a discreetly lowered voice, "This is probably not the right time to bring it up, but…how'd it go with Ray?"

"You're right," Ben said, not unkindly, "it's not the right time. But given the circumstances, I'd have to say it went very well." Quinn nodded, squeezing Ben's arm now, tears brimming on his lower lids. Ben said, "I'll tell you all about it later, okay, Ed?" and Quinn nodded, drying his eyes on his sleeve.

* * *

Hugging the wall, Quinn crept Ninja-like along the narrow corridor leading to the staff parking lot. At six-foot-six, Quinn was by far the tallest of the group, and when he got to the exit, it was a small matter for him to slip one of his size-fourteen gym socks over the lens of the security camera.

Seconds later, all four stood in a cluster at the glass door, gazing out at Hicks's cherry-red Mercedes, ten feet away in its private spot.

Breathing hard, Quinn whispered, "How'd you end up with the dink's key?"

"It's a long story," Ben said. "And you don't have to whisper. There's no audio on the cameras." He chuckled then, looking at the fancy key. "I was going to toss it in the garbage, screw up the bastard's night even more. But this is so much better."

Wilder said, "When's the last time you drove a car?"

"When Adam was a boy scout."

Viktor said, "We're all gonna die," and the men shared a conspiratorial chuckle.

Ben aimed the key through the glass and thumbed the little 'unlock' button, a dim interior light coming on in the car. Now he said, "Ready?" and pushed the door open, setting off a strident alarm.

A few seconds later the men were in the car, Ben scrambling to find the ignition, Quinn saying, "Push the green button, push the green *button*."

Then they were away, Ben laying rubber in a wild half-donut, Wilder whooping in the back seat. Ben got the powerful vehicle aimed at the exit, praying the barricade would lift—then it did, and in a small, pained voice in the shotgun seat Viktor said, "Turn right. And step on it. I can't feel my prick anymore."

* * *

Leaning forward in the back seat, Quinn said, "Think Hicks'll call the cops?"

"I can almost guarantee he won't," Ben said, hanging a right off Bronson onto Sunnyside, then a quick left onto Bronson Place, the street Ray had grown up on. The house was still there, perched on the hill, looking pretty much as it had sixty years ago. Ben slowed to study it as they passed, then took the ramp back onto Bronson and the bridge over the Rideau Canal. He exited Bronson at Fifth Avenue and followed it to Bank Street, then turned left toward the Byward Market, thirty blocks away now, dead ahead.

Traffic was scant at this hour, just a lone pickup truck trailing them, and Ben was beginning to enjoy the quiet responsiveness of the German-engineered vehicle, his earlier fatigue melting away.

Now Wilder said, "Hey, Vik, how's it hanging?"

"Hurts."

"I imagine," Wilder said. "Listen, I've been meaning to ask. What's the attraction with these supersize gals?"

"My first true love was a big girl," Viktor said. "I was fifteen, she was twenty. Nadia. We did it in the loft of her father's hay barn. She was very warm." He gave a pained chuckle. "And she could handle the equipment. I tried skinny girls too, lots of them. But it was like I was impaling them, not pleasuring them. And big girls are very grateful."

Wilder said, "So what does a ride on one these up-town blimps cost?"

Viktor flinched as if shot. "Oh, shit, we have to go back."

Ben said, "What for?"

"I forgot my wallet."

Wilder laughed. "Oh, that's perfect." He looked at Quinn. "Hey, Ed, you gonna cover it for him?" And to Viktor. "How much for this little hayride, comrade?"

Wincing, Viktor said, "Five hundred."

The other three in unison: "*Dollars*?"

Viktor turned in his seat, the look on his face the most pathetic Ben had ever seen. Glancing at his wrist-watch, Viktor said, "Come on, guys, there's no *time* to go back. Can you lend me the money? Please? I'll pay you back, you have my word."

Grumbling, all three men checked their pockets, com-ing up with a total of eight dollars and forty cents.

Wilder said, "She won't even let you say hi to the thing for that amount of money."

"Mean bastard," Quinn said. "Anyone bring a Visa or ATM card?"

Wilder shook his head. Ben said, "My wallet's on the dresser at home," and Viktor slumped in his seat, de-spondent.

At Lisgar Street, halfway to the Byward Market, a bearded wino stumbled into the street, looking like Death itself in the glare of the headlights. Ben stomped on the brakes—and felt a jarring impact from behind, all three of his passengers shouting in alarm now, beer from Wilder's king can spraying the back of Ben's neck.

Bugging his eyes at the Mercedes, the wino kept going, and Ben looked in the rearview to see the pickup buried in their ass, hood crumpled, rad hissing steam.

Quinn said, "Oh, this is just great. We are well and truly *screwed* now. We're all going to *jail*."

In a dead-sober voice, Wilder said, "Let me handle this," and got out of the car.

* * *

Ben watched Wilder approach the driver's side of the pickup. He had little doubt the man could handle himself in a scrap, even at seventy-seven years of age. He'd never met a stronger guy. Wilder's perpetually baggy clothing concealed a hundred and seventy-five pounds of wiry Anglo Saxon muscle. But still, he was worried, tempted to dial 911 on the car phone, get the cops down here pronto and deal with the consequences later.

Then he saw the driver's door open back there and a scrawny guy in his forties stumble out onto the street. The guy was clearly inebriated, gesturing angrily at Wilder now, and Ben was afraid it would come to blows.

Quinn said, "You think we should go help him?"

Now Wilder had the guy by the throat, backing him up against the quarter panel of the truck, pointing at the Royal Bank across the street.

Ben said, "What the hell?" and watched Wilder lead the guy to a row of ATM machines in the outer lobby of the bank.

A few minutes later, Wilder was back in the car, saying, "How much did you say you needed?" The grimacing Russian showed him five fingers and Wilder peeled ten crisp fifties off the pile. Handing over the cash, he said, "Now drive," to Ben and pocketed the rest.

Ben punched the accelerator. The vehicle balked at first, as if restrained by a giant hand. Then it peeled away with a hellish screech of metal against metal. As they fishtailed down the street, Ben glanced in the rearview and saw the pickup driver looking after them, scratching his booze-addled head.

Laughing, Quinn said, "How did you pull *that* off?"

"I reminded the asshole that in the eyes of the law, rear-ending us would be considered his fault. Then I asked him how he thought he'd make out on a breathalyzer test. Guy smelled like a brewery. I told him my friend was in our very expensive vehicle right now dialing 911 and the poor bastard said, 'How much damage you think we're talking about here?' So I asked him what his withdrawal limit was."

"Sneaky prick," Quinn said, gazing at Wilder with open admiration. "How much did you get?"

"None of your business."

Clutching the fifties, Viktor said, "Go left on Bruyère Street. And please hurry."

* * *

The car phone rang as Ben braked in front of a non-descript building, *Rubens* in pink neon flashing above the unlit entrance. He could see on call-display it was the CEO, and he thumbed the receiver button, raising a finger to silence the others. Before he could say hello, Hicks's voice blared through the speakers, loud enough to make Ben flinch: "Hunter, you demented old weasel, you get my fucking Mercedes back here *right now*, and maybe, just *may*be, I won't have you killed."

Ben hung up.

Wilder said, "He sounds upset," and Ben had to laugh.

Turning in his seat, Ben said, "Why don't you guys take Viktor inside." He was getting into the sheer delinquency of the evening now, knowing in his heart if Ray were here he'd be cheering them on. Sure, Hicks was pissed, but Ben had him by the short hairs now, and no amount of red-faced fury was going to change that. Not ever. He was halfway inclined to drive the car into the alley over there and set it on fire. But they needed a ride home.

The boys were on the sidewalk now, propping up the hobbled Russian.

Ben said, "I'll park this thing and meet you inside. And Viktor, try not to cripple the poor girl."

Viktor managed a pained grin.

* * *

As he entered Rubens, which was really just a thinly-disguised cathouse, Ben was assaulted by blaring pop music and rank humidity. He spotted his friends huddled next to a huge plastic knockoff of a sculpture by Fernando Botero called *Reclining Woman*. Quinn was fondling the thing's globular breasts, pretending to be transported with passion.

Ben thought, *Dummy's going to get us thrown out.* He said, "Where's Viktor?"

Quinn pointed at the ceiling, saying, "Loosing the Georgian giant," and all of them laughed.

They got a table near the exit, Wilder saying he didn't want to get too close to the waitresses in case one of them fell on him. The smallest in the room ran maybe two-ninety, all of them attired in stiletto heels, pink-leather thongs, and pasties the size of dinner plates.

Shaking his head, Ben said, "Must be an acquired taste."

But the place was packed, mostly with skinny dudes in their forties, working men hooting at mammoth dancers turning slow revolutions around reinforced stripper poles, dust sifting down from the ceiling when the moves got too ambitious. It was hard to look at and even harder to look away.

A waitress plodded up to the table now and Wilder shrank back in mock alarm. The girl said, "Cute. My name's Mindy, what can I get youse?"

The guys ordered beers and Mindy lumbered away, Ed pointing at her dimpled can as she oozed between tables, heading for the bar. "Hail damage," he said, and got a laugh out of Wilder.

Ben sighed, feeling the fatigue again now, dully awed by the freak show around him. He wondered how Viktor was making out upstairs.

* * *

It was the same room from the video chats. Same vast bed, same picture above the headboard, a faded print of Peter Paul Rubens' *The Hermit and the Sleeping Angelica*, the painting an apt accessory to what lay ahead on this magical night: the ancient hermit kneeling at the bedside, the amply proportioned Angelica reclining in naked slumber.

Except *his* angel was flesh and blood and wideawake, smiling now, stretching a bright slash of crimson into a stack of chins.

As he stepped through the doorway, she propped up her massive head, crooning, "What are you waiting for, sweet Viktor? Your hour begins now."

Fingers betraying him, Viktor wrestled with the knot on his sweatpants, turning his back on the girl to get the job done. Then he had it and he let the pants drop, baring his skinny ass, almost falling when he caught his heel on the cuff bending to yank the damn things off.

Breathing hard, he faced her now, hearing her gasp at the sight of him. Smile widening, Lisa raised those stately arms, saying, "Come here, my sweet Soviet sex machine. Let me help you with that thing."

Repeating the words, "Oh boy, oh boy, oh boy," like some arcane fertility chant, Viktor climbed aboard, Lisa's pillowy thighs parting to receive him. With a sigh of relief, he sank into a buttery mass of musk and heat and unspeakable delights.

* * *

The Russian didn't say much on the drive home, only smiled and nodded, discouraging the rude comments from the back seat. Before long he fell fast asleep, head lolling against the window, the fearsome bulge in his pants at last subsided.

They found Hicks sitting on the curb by his executive parking spot, dark eyes flashing red in the sweep of headlights as Ben guided the Mercedes into its slot. The men bailed out as Ben killed the engine, Ben the only one with stones enough to look the man in the eye. Handing Hicks the key, he said, "Thanks for the loan of the vehicle, Cliff. She handles like a dream." Without a word, Hicks snatched the key and opened the car door.

Entering the building now, Ben said, "Sorry about the ding on the trunk," and pulled the door shut. Through the soundproof glass, the men watched Hicks stride to the back of the vehicle to gape in horror at the damage: the rear end staved in, his expensive golf clubs bristling from the sprung trunk like bent quills. Laughing, they watched the red-faced CEO yank out one of the clubs and fling it as far as he could into the parking lot, laughing even harder when the twirling nine iron arrowed through the windshield of a maintenance van.

Sparing them a final, venomous glare, Hicks scrambled into the Mercedes and got the hell out of there.

ELEVEN

Wednesday, July 12

BEYOND EXHAUSTED NOW, BEN settled into the La-Z-Boy with the TV on, mauve dawnlight tinting the windows behind him. The Cecile B. DeMille classic *The Ten Commandments* was playing, and as the fatigue had its way with him, Ben remembered seeing the film with Melanie in the seventies. They'd seen a lot of movies together in those days, sitting high in the balcony of the Capitol Theater, munching popcorn and necking during the slow parts. *Sometimes even the good parts*, Ben thought, and licked his lips, tasting the peach-flavored lip balm she always wore.

Eyelids drooping, he remembered something else about that long-ago matinee. Holding his lover's hand as Moses parted the Red Sea, he'd begun to weep for reasons he still couldn't fathom. Perhaps it had stemmed from his conflicted Catholic upbringing, or from his cold certainty by this point that his relationship with Melanie was on the skids. Whatever it was, the upset had been profound and uncontrollable. Afterward, Melanie had told him she understood, but he'd never pressed her to explain her take on the experience. She'd broken it off with him a few months later, telling him she'd met someone else. That someone had sired her only child, and abandoned her on the day she went into labor. She'd met her second husband a few years later.

Losing Melanie had undone him. He'd been halfway through second-year med school when it happened, just days before a classmate took his own life with an ampoule of potassium chloride, leaving a scrawled note that read, *It's too much*. And in that first dark stretch without the girl he'd hoped to marry, that simple phrase had reverberated with seductive regularity in his mind, a clarion call from an inner abyss along the crumbling margin of which he would wander for the next two years. It was only the increasing demands of academic life—and the faint hope Melanie might one day take him back—that kept him from toppling over the edge. He'd filled the hole as best he could: pot, alcohol, and the kind of reckless promiscuity good looks, a leather med-school jacket and playing in a rock band made possible. But it wasn't until his first year of residency that the wounds began to heal, and a livable future began to take shape.

Ben slept now, tumbling into the dream that had cost him his supper the night before. Only this time when the girl beneath him swept the hair off her face, it was Melanie.

* * *

Voices.

Familiar voices...

"Is he gone again?"

"Again? He was out of it when we got here."

"What was that shit he was going on about? Moses? The Red Sea?"

"Hell if I know."

Ben thought, *Wilder?* and opened his eyes on a strange room, thinking, *What a bizarre dream.* There were two old men standing over him now, leaning in to view him as if he were laid out in an open coffin. One of them, the wiry one, had Vince Wilder's voice—

"His eyes are open now."

And the other one sounded like Quinn.

"Ben?"

Now Wilder's voice again.

"Lights are on but nobody's home."

"Should we call an ambulance?"

"What's the point? He's breathing. Maybe he'll be back, maybe he won't."

"I don't know, Vince. I think we should call somebody. Have him seen."

"Do what you want, but it's half-past suppertime and I'm hungry."

"*Come on, man, let's just hang here a while. See what he does.*"

Ben closed his eyes and looked at Melanie, sound asleep on the bunk bed beside him. He hoped those two old farts would go away before they woke her up.

Eventually, they did.

* * *

Knocking.

Go away.

Knocking again...and now ringing. Insistent in his ear.

The phone.

Ben opened his eyes and grabbed the receiver off the end table next to the La-Z-Boy.

"Yes?"

"Hi, Ben, it's me."

"Melanie?"

"No, it's Roxanne. Are you all right?"

"Yeah, yeah. I guess I was sleeping." He peered around the apartment. Shadows everywhere, the only light from the muted TV. He said, "I thought I heard knocking."

"That was me."

"What?"

She said, "I'm outside your door," and laughed, the sound strained, no real humor in it. "I just finished my shift. Quinn told me you'd probably still be up. Can I come in?"

He said, "Of course, gimme a sec," and began worming his way out of the La-Z-Boy. When he'd made it into a sitting position, he brought the phone back to his ear. "Roxanne? Still there?"

She giggled, the sound more genuine now. "Yes."

"Okay, almost there."

He lowered his feet to the floor and stood, wondering how long he'd been angled into that chair. A glance at his watch told him it was 9:18 PM, so at least fifteen hours. His last recollection was of Moses parting the Rea Sea.

Shit.

Had he been dreaming?

In the foyer he switched on the lights and glanced in the mirror, saying into the phone, "Brace yourself, kid. I look like Herman Munster."

He heard her say, "Herman who?" and let her in.

Eyes widening, Roxanne said, "Yikes," and tucked her phone away, telling him he smelled like a gym sock.

Ben said, "Keeps the flies off the ice cream," and latched the door behind her. He said, "You'll have to excuse me a minute. Gotta see a man about a dog."

He could still taste peach lip balm on his lips.

* * *

While she waited for Ben's return, Roxanne got some tea brewing: Orange Pekoe, Ben's favorite, the individual bags stacked in a porcelain dispenser on the kitchen counter. She loved how *neat* his apartment was, everything arranged just so. She'd never want him to see her bedroom. A neat-freak she wasn't. Russ had actually flinched when he saw it, Gram ambushing her the other day, bringing him upstairs when he came by to pick her up instead of making him wait in the family room. Another of Gram's good-natured—if pointless—attempts at getting her to organize her things.

She arranged the teapot, cups and spoons on a tray and carried it into the living room, setting it on the coffee table as Ben came back into the room.

Rubbing his hands together, he said, "I *thought* I smelled something delicious. Thanks, Roxie. There's some tea biscuits in the breadbox if you're hungry."

Roxanne said, "No thank you, Doctor Hunter," and they sat together on the couch, sipping hot brew. They made small talk for a while, Roxanne giving him the highlights of her shift, making special reference to the fragrant load the bird lady had deposited in her bed, adding, "It looked like she'd been sampling the birdseed herself." Doing his best to be discrete, Ben told her about Viktor's late-night dilemma and got her laughing so hard she almost wet herself. When he was done, she said, "I didn't know you had a car," and Ben told her he didn't, but that was a whole other story.

Pouring more tea now, Ben said, "So to what do I owe the pleasure?"

"I bumped into Quinn earlier and he told me about your friend Ray."

Ben set his teacup on the table. Not unkindly, he said, "You could park a Winnebago in that man's mouth."

"He also said he and Wilder were here earlier and you seemed a little…out of it. I just wanted to make sure you were okay."

Almost inaudibly, Ben said, "So I wasn't dreaming," but Roxanne decided to let that part of it go. He seemed fine now and that was all that mattered.

She said, "Are you going to be in any trouble?"

"Hmm?"

"You know. For the thing with Ray?"

Ben said, "No. Other than dragging around a broken heart for a while, it's all under control."

Roxanne wasn't so sure she believed him, but he seemed genuine enough. She wanted to ask how he'd gotten away with it—she knew he'd retired years ago, and was fairly certain his license to practice medicine would have long since expired—but she decided to let that go, too. She said, "You guys were close, huh."

Ben said, "Best friends since the third grade," and spent the better part of an hour describing some of their antics growing up, getting her laughing again. Then he told her about their final moments together and she cried along with him.

It was jarring, seeing him grieve. He'd been a rock to her since the day they met—even when he got confused about who she was—and she was grateful for the chance to return the favor, Ben resting his head against her shoulder now instead of the other way around.

After a while, he begged off to the bathroom again. Roxanne told him to light a match, she had to go too, and that got a chuckle out of him.

Once they'd both done their business, Roxanne toasted an English muffin for each of them and warmed up the tea in the microwave. They sat at the kitchen table this time, and Roxanne said, "So what was it like seeing Gram again?"

Ben smiled—a little dreamily, Roxanne thought—saying, "It was wonderful. I'd forgotten how beautiful she is."

"Aw."

"Did she say anything? About me?"

"Just that it was nice seeing you again," Roxanne said, praying her poker face was holding up. She wasn't lying—Gram *had* seemed pleased to see him—but she wasn't about to tell him what she'd said later that day.

Sounding disappointed, Ben said, "That was it?"

"Gram can be pretty close-mouthed."

"I remember."

"And stubborn."

"I remember that, too."

"I tried to get her to tell me about you two, but she brushed me off. Said it was a long time ago."

Ben said, "What do you want to know?"

"All of it."

* * *

And that was exactly what he told her. He started with the first time he'd set eyes on Melanie Anderson in the hallway at Hillcrest High, and finished with the phone call that ended them six years later.

"I didn't realize I was screwing it up until it was too late. I *thought* I was building a future for us, setting the stage for a marriage proposal." He smiled. "I still have the ring and the airline tickets. I was going to pop the question in Hawaii.

"But what I was really doing was putting her last. Behind my studies, behind the guys I hung out with, behind my compulsion to be at the top of my class. She met her first husband while I was doing a locum in Edmonton. Met him in a grocery store—" Ben felt suddenly stricken. "Oh, sweetie, please tell me you already know about this."

Roxanne nodded. "Gram told me when I turned fourteen. Bastard left her while she was pregnant with my mom. It's all right, Ben."

He thought, *Thank God.* "She broke it off with me over the phone. I begged for another chance, said I could do better, even told her I'd drop out of med school if that was what it took. But it was too late. I'd lost her. It got pathetic for a while after that. I still had a week left in the locum, but after she hung up on me, I got in my car and drove back to Ottawa. Twenty-two-hundred miles. Flat out for forty hours, only stopping for junk food and gas. To this day, I can't remember long stretches of that trip. I'm pretty sure I drove through the prairies sound asleep. And I damned near got *kicked* out of med school for taking off from the locum without letting anyone know.

"I caught up with her where she worked."

"Le Château, right?"

"That's right. Hippest clothing store in Ottawa at the time." He shuddered. "Jesus. I stumbled in there in the middle of her shift, barely conscious from the drive. Hadn't bathed, shaved or changed clothes in three days. And she was *so* beautiful. Decked out in a pink one-piece, stacking sweaters on a display. And the look she gave me when she saw me...I wanted to die. Startled at first. Then just...nothing. Like I was something she'd have to sweep up."

Roxanne touched his arm, and when he looked at her in the warm apartment light he thought she was Melanie. But only for an eyeblink.

"I spent the next six months trying to win her back. But all I was doing was making it worse. After she threatened to call the cops the next time I rang her door-bell, I finally accepted it was over."

"Wow. Gram's even tougher than I thought."

"She was just protecting herself. And she was right. I never would've changed. For a while maybe, to get her back. But I was so *driven* in those days, Roxanne. Had to be the best at everything.

"Anyway, it was a disaster. So I put my head down and carried on. Got my ticket in anesthesia—don't ask me why, the work never suited me—and did the job for three years before going back to study geriatrics. I dated, sure. Even lived with a girl for a while. But the vulnerable part of me your grandmother reached, that part went deep. After Mel, I was only going through the motions with women. Commitment never entered my mind. After your grandmother, it was all about the work."

He smiled now, trying to make light of it.

Roxanne said, "Ben, that is so sad."

"It's just life, sweetheart. You make the best of the hand you're dealt."

"And what about now?"

"What about now what?"

"What about taking another shot?"

"What do you mean?"

Roxanne gave him a gentle poke. "Come on, *Benjamin*, don't play dumb with me. I saw your face when you realized who she was. And when she hugged you? I thought you were going to faint dead away."

He could feel himself blushing again. *Damn it.* "That obvious, huh?"

"Neon *sign* obvious."

"Well, here's the thing, Roxanne. People seldom change. Particularly one as iron-willed as your grandmother. And while I'm certain she believes in second chances, I know her well enough to know that particular door was barricaded shut decades ago. I practically wore her out trying to pry it open. And when she hugged me on the porch the other day, I could tell nothing had changed. That anger, that *wariness*, was still there, just below the surface. I'm willing to wager she only put up with me being there because she could see how much you and I mean to each other. And I got lost a couple of times that day, kiddo. I'm sure she noticed. I know you did."

"Ben..."

"Tell me I'm wrong. Better yet, tell me what she really said when you two talked about it later."

* * *

Roxanne thought, *Put your foot in it this time, girl.* But he deserved to know. She said, "You have to remember what she's like. When she's upset, she re*acts*, and sometimes what comes out of her mouth can be hurtful."

Nodding, Ben said, "So what did she say?"

Roxanne could feel her face getting red, and hated that about herself more in this moment than at any other time in her life. She thought, *Just say it.* "She told me there's no way she's getting involved with you again. She said the fact that you and I are friends is fine, and because of that she'd be okay with you coming over from time to time. Said she'd even do things with us if she was invited."

"But bottom line, she's not interested."

Seeing a way to put a positive spin on it, Roxanne said, "That big doctor's brain in there and you *still* don't understand women?"

"What do you mean?"

"She was upset because I ambushed her, bringing you over without letting her know."

"So what part don't I understand?"

"The fact she was up*set*. If seeing you again was no big deal, then I'd be agreeing with you. No chance with Gram."

"So the fact she was upset...?"

"Oh, my *God*. Am I gonna have to lead you by the hand?"

Smirking, Ben thought, *Ask your grandmother about that*. He said, "Lead on."

Roxanne took a quick slurp of tea. "Okay. She was upset, but she said you're welcome at the house anytime and that she'd love to tag along."

"That's stretching it a bit, don't you think?"

"Not at all." *Now comes the hard part.* "But you were right about one thing. She *did* notice your...lapses the other day. And she said straight out she's too old to get stuck in a care-giving role again."

"Did you tell her about the isomer?"

"I did. Sold it pretty hard, in fact."

"Did you tell her it hasn't had time to work yet?"

Roxanne nodded.

"So that's it, then."

Roxanne thought, *Yeah, that's probably it*. But she said, "Not necessarily. I think what she needs now is time. We've got the rest of the summer. Let her see you around, but keep it cool with her. Friends only. She'll see us having fun and she'll want to join in. Plus, she'll see you getting better on the medication. In the meantime, I'll keep working on her." She smiled. "I'm an excellent matchmaker."

Ben shook his head and returned her smile, saying, "Women."

Roxanne poked him again.

PART THREE

TWELVE

ROXANNE LEFT FOR HALIFAX on Friday, August 28th, the air on that blustery morning rank with the promise of autumn. A thunderstorm broke while they waited for the Air Canada desk to announce her flight, and Ben half-hoped her departure would be delayed. But the squall passed as quickly as it came. He kept stealing glances at Melanie, certain when the moment came she was going to break down, which all but guaranteed he would, too.

Still in their windbreakers, they sat at a beverage kiosk with a view of the airfield, sipping coffee and trying to pretend this wasn't the saddest day ever. Ben could see Roxanne was excited, but he could read the concern in her eyes, too. This would be the first time she'd been away from her grandmother for more than a week at a stretch, and Ben knew she couldn't bear the thought of the old woman alone in that house.

The security alert for the Halifax flight came at 7:00 AM, and Roxanne stood, saying, "That's me," with a trembling smile.

Melanie's eyes shimmered as she got to her feet, and Ben said to Roxanne, "Why don't we walk you to the gate?" trying to put off the tears as long as he could.

He slung Roxanne's carry-on over his shoulder, and the trio began a somber trek to the security area, footfalls echoing off the high, latticework ceiling.

The lineup at the security checkpoint was moving briskly this morning, and when they were ten feet from the entrance Roxanne said, "We should probably say our goodbyes now." As predicted, a big fat tear rolled down Melanie's cheek, and Roxanne followed suit, wrapping her arms around her grandmother and holding on tight. Watching them, Ben lost it too. But they were *good* tears, filled with love and hope and fond wishes.

After murmuring to her grandmother for a moment—telling her everything was going to be fine, she'd call the instant the plane touched down in Halifax—Roxanne held an arm out to Ben, inviting him into the circle. Ben joined in gratefully, intoxicated by the unexpected contact with Melanie, her smooth hip warm against his thigh. He gasped softly when she slung an arm around his waist, drawing him closer with surprising strength, and he wanted to stand there forever with these people he loved so much.

But an impatient woman in a severe blue security uniform was waving Roxanne over now, and they backed away from each other. Ben handed Roxanne her bag and Melanie moved in to plant a final kiss on her forehead.

Starting away, Roxanne said, "You guys should probably just head home. You can't go any further with me, and the plane doesn't leave for another hour."

The security guard said, "Miss?"

And Roxanne was gone.

* * *

They returned to the city in silence, Melanie discouraging Ben's attempts at small talk with soft grunts and one-word answers. Fearful of upsetting her further, he decided to hold his tongue. Mel was nothing if not tough, but he could see losing Roxanne had stretched that toughness to its limit. And he knew from long-past experience, the best thing he could do now was to give her space.

She pulled up in front of his building at a quarter to eight, the only sound the cadenced back-and-forth of the wiper blades, working against the drizzle. He thanked her, shifted his body to climb out—and felt Mel's warm hand on top of his.

She said, "I'm sorry, Ben. It's been a rough day and it's not even eight o'clock yet." She gave him a thin smile. "I like that we're friends again, and I want to spend time with you. But today, I just need to be alone. I'm going to go home, have a cup of tea and sit in my chair with a good book."

"Tolkien?"

Melanie laughed. "Probably."

"Can I call you?"

"Please do. But give it a few days, okay? I prefer to feel sorry for myself in private."

"I will. And try not to worry, Mel. Roxanne's a smart, sensible girl, and this really is the best thing for—"

She gave him a look that said, *Tell me something I don't already know*, and Ben buttoned his lip. He said, "I'll call you," and got out in the rain. He stood a moment, watching her drive away, the brake lights on her sporty Civic spilling red on the slick pavement as she obeyed the stop sign.

Then she was gone, too.

Ben went inside, his hand still warm where Melanie had touched it.

* * *

He could hear the phone from outside the door, and his first thought was *Melanie*. He fumbled the key code a few times, attributing the lapse to his eagerness to get to the phone—then he was inside, winded, grabbing the receiver so urgently he almost dropped it on the floor.

"Mel?"

"No, Ben, it's Jake."

Ben thought, *Jake?* Then he remembered.

"Ben, you still there?"

"Yes."

"Listen, I've only got a minute, but I'm afraid I've got some bad news. It's about the isomer; it's stopped working. We're not certain yet, but we believe it's a receptor problem. The results were encouraging at first, as you know, but in the past few days it's all gone to hell. In about ten percent of the study patients, the drug appears to have exacerbated the dementia. And there've been some issues with cardiotoxicity. Two patients have had infarcts, Ben, one of them fatal. So you need to get off the stuff, okay? And I want you to get some bloodwork done. Troponins, electrolytes, CBC, renal and hepatic panels. I think you'll be fine, since you entered the study a month behind the others, but better safe than sorry."

"I see."

"I apologize, Ben. I got your hopes up for nothing. It's back to the drawing board for the isomer, I'm afraid."

"Well, I think you're way off base on this one, Jake. I feel amazing. Clear as a bell. All I've had is a little indigestion, and I'm more inclined to blame that on cafeteria food than the isomer. I'm right as rain."

"I don't have time to discuss it now," Jake said. "I'm in London on a conference gig and I'm already late for my talk. But I need you to trust me on this, okay? Stop the medication. Get rid of it. I'll be back in the country in a week. We can talk more then."

"I'm right as rain."

"Stop the medication, Ben. I've got to sign off. I'll call you next week."

Ben listened to the dial tone for a moment, then hung up. He was glad Jake had called. He'd almost forgotten to take his medication.

* * *

Roxanne cried some more on the plane. Ben had surprised her with a business-class ticket on the sleek Bombardier CRJ9 domestic jet, and she'd been lucky enough to score a seat in the row of singles on the port side of the aircraft. It wasn't exactly private, but at least there was no one bumping elbows with her, and she could turn her face to the window and hide in her hair. She wished Russ could have joined her for the trip, but he'd been forced to leave a week earlier to secure the off-campus apartment he'd be sharing with the guys in his band.

Roxanne dried her eyes and gazed out at the morning sky. She was already homesick. But what was upsetting her most was the thought of Gram alone in that house. Every time she blinked she saw the old woman tumbling down the basement steps or slipping in the shower or lying dead from a stroke on the kitchen floor. Now more than ever she wished she'd pushed Gram harder to sell the house and move into the Center. Ben had done his best to convince her too, taking her on an hour-long tour of the complex, then treating her to lunch in the cafeteria while extolling the many virtues of assisted living.

But Gram could be so pigheaded. Once her mind was made up, there was seldom any changing it. And the harder you pushed, the more stubbornly she hunkered down. Which made Roxanne think of something else that concerned her almost as much.

Ben still had his heart set on getting back with Gram. But barring divine intervention—or a small stroke in the willful part of Gram's brain—Roxanne was convinced now that it was never going to happen. In spite of Ben's best efforts, Gram had remained cool toward him all summer. Slinging her arm around him at the airport was the warmest thing she'd done since that very first hug on the porch. And Ben had been knocking himself out trying to woo her: flowers coming out of the blue, lavish dinners, shiny gifts in tiny packages, movie dates in the theater they'd favored in their teens. All to little avail.

Roxanne still loved the idea, though, and a part of her clung to the frail hope Gram was only playing hard to get. Either way, she'd continue trying to soften the old girl up. They deserved to be together. Even Russ thought it was the most romantic thing he'd ever heard, first lovers reuniting after sixty years, sharing the balance of their lives in a quaint riverside home.

Maybe even having *sex*.

Roxanne giggled at this forbidden thought, peeking through her hair now to see a surly woman eyeballing her from across the aisle.

She faced the window again—a quiltwork of fields beneath her now, dotted with the occasional homestead—and recalled the mid-August afternoon she'd spent with Ben at his winterized cottage in Constance Bay. They'd borrowed Gram's car that day, and Ben told her he hadn't visited the property in ages, but paid a local fellow a monthly stipend to maintain it.

The 'cottage' turned out to be a plush two-bedroom chalet perched high on a wooded rise, with a breezy deck overlooking the Ottawa River and a railed, flagstone staircase zigzagging down to a sandy beach. Roxanne had spent the afternoon helping Ben spruce the place up, cracking a few windows to flush out the stale air, running a vacuum through the rooms, Swiffer-dusting the antique furniture. Afterward, they'd dined on the deck, munching fish and chips from a nearby chip wagon, then watched the sun sizzle into the bay in a spectacular blush of fuchsia and furnace red.

And it was here Ben told her of his plan to propose to Gram with the ring he'd purchased back in 1972. Roxanne told him outright what a *bad* idea that was, almost blurting it, telling him Gram was nowhere near ready for anything as radical as marriage, and probably never would be.

But Ben was adamant.

"I think she's ready," he told her, sipping the dregs of the Pepsi he'd had with dinner.

Not wanting to hurt his feelings any more than she already had, Roxanne said, "What makes you so sure?"

"I can just tell."

"Have you discussed it with her yet?"

He laughed, and not for the first time Roxanne wondered if the isomer was still doing its job. He'd been rock solid for the past month, but now....

He said, "Are you *crazy*? You know what she's like."

"So what, you're just going to spring it on her?"

"Ex*a*ctly. I mean, that's why we're here today, to get the place ready. I'm going to invite her up for dinner—I was thinking a week or so after you leave, give her time to realize how crappy living alone can be. We'll dine by candlelight, chat about the good times we had. And when the time is right, I'll pop the question." He smiled. "What do you think?"

"Gram doesn't like surprises. Even good ones."

"What's not to like? And there'll be no pressure to, you know... There's two bedrooms upstairs; she can have the big one. I'll do all the cooking. There's a grocery store within walking distance, a hospital ten minutes' drive away, and I've already found a cleaning lady willing to come in a couple times a week. There's cell and Internet access, and all the movies and TV shows a person could want. And she can read her Tolkien right out here on the deck." He indicated the rocker Roxanne was sitting in. "Recognize the chair?" It was an exact duplicate of Gram's. "I had it shipped to the caretaker last week. And I've decided to write a memoir in that little office out back, so I won't be in her hair much at all.

"I love her, Roxanne. I never stopped loving her. I just kind of...tucked it away. No one's more surprised than I am at how quickly the years flew by. But one of the last things Ray said to me before he died was that I should go for it. So that's what I'm going to do."

He'd gotten quiet then, giving her that feeling of absence, and Roxanne wondered again if his meds were still working.

But it was out of her hands now, all of it, and she felt a certain lightness because of it. Brushing the hair out of her eyes, she glanced back along the jet's plush interior, thinking, *I'm really doing it.*

And as the miles stacked up behind her, she felt herself on the cusp of adulthood, of *woman*hood, and sensed a dormant spirit of adventure stirring inside her.

She settled back with a sigh, eyes aimed straight ahead.

* * *

Ben waited three full days before calling. It was torture.

"Hello?"

"Hi, Melanie."

"I'm sorry. Who is this?"

"It's Ben."

"I know that, silly boy. What's on your mind?"

"I'm feeling like a walk in the park, and I thought you might like to join me."

A hesitant sigh. "It's almost lunchtime, Ben, and I've got chores. I'm not sure I want to drive all the way out there right now."

"Not the park here. The park there."

"Here? You mean Brown's Inlet?"

"Uh huh."

"You don't have a car."

"I'll take the bus."

"Benjamin Hunter, MD, take the *bus*?"

"Sure. Why not? It'll be fun. And it'll give you time to have lunch and put on something nice."

She giggled and Ben felt lightheaded.

She said, "I know what you're up to."

"Oh, you do, do you."

"Yes, I do."

"So meet me and try to stop me."

She huffed. "I'm not making any promises. What time were you thinking?"

"There's a bus leaving here in twelve minutes." He glanced at his watch. "An hour from now at the weeping willow?"

She chuckled. "Now I *really* know what you're up to. God, I haven't thought of that place in ages."

"I'll see you there, then?"

"That old tree was ready to fall into the pond when we were kids. What if it's gone?"

"Then I'll meet you where it used to be."

"I'm not promising anything."

"There'll be ice cream."

"Ben Hunter, you *dirty* old man."

He hung up on their laughter, then hurried out to the bus stop at the curb.

* * *

The bus was packed and reeked of b.o. Myriad other odors assaulted Ben as he stumbled along the aisle, lurching from handhold to handhold as the driver tramped on the gas: curry; garlic; stale booze; a fart so nasty he could feel the heat of it on his face; cotton candy; cheap perfume; the lingering stench of spent cigarettes.

There wasn't a seat to be had, so he grabbed a chrome stanchion and held on for dear life, doing his best to avoid colliding with the other straphangers. The jerky motion was already playing hell with his joints.

He thought, *Should've called a cab*, and tried to calm himself with thoughts of the day ahead.

A seat came up a few stops later, but just as Ben moved to claim it, a pair of pierced, tattooed, rail-thin teenagers dove in, lapsing into a tangle of roaming hands and flickering tongues. Ben had to turn his back to avoid laughing out loud.

I guess I don't get out enough.

He was facing a young man in a suit now, and when the bus lurched again the man said, "Can I offer you my seat, sir?"

Ben thought, *'Sir', I get it, I'm old*, although the truth of it often caught him unawares. He said, "No thanks, I'll manage," and stumbled again.

The young man stood now, blocking another couple of hard-looking kids with his body. He said, "It would be my honor, Doctor Hunter."

"You know who I am?"

The man nodded. "I'm a resident in internal medicine. I've read all of your papers." He touched Ben's elbow, guiding him into the seat. "I've even read one of
your thrillers. *Code Blue*. Loved it. I've had your novels
on my reader for ages, just haven't had time to enjoy
them all yet."

Ben felt proud as a peacock. He wanted to ask the
young man if he'd rotated through the Geriatric Center
yet, maybe offer to buy him lunch next time he was
there. But the bus came to a chuffing stop and the young
man said, "This is me."

Ben thanked him for the seat and watched him dis-
embark, the four teens plowing through the narrow exit
ahead of him.

Then the bus was rolling again, heading north on
Bronson at a lively clip, the big wheels humming a sop-
orific note. Lulled by it, Ben went away for a while.

* * *

He disembarked at the corner of Ralph and Wood-
lawn and walked the short city block to Brown's Inlet, a
long, kidney-shaped pond teeming with catfish and
toads. Ralph Street split the pond in half, and it was to
the most easterly of these fragrant lagoons Ben made his
way now, leaving the sidewalk to follow a dirt path to
the ancient willow. The tortured tree still clung to the
undercut bank, and still looked ready to teeter into the
pond. The trunk jutted out from the bank at a steep angle for a good six feet, then leveled off into a flattened

bench just wide enough for two before angling upward to its full height of perhaps thirty feet.

In his childhood, Ben had spent many a summer day here with Ray, netting tadpoles or fishing for mudpout, balanced high on their secret perch, secure within the screening canopy. They'd rarely caught anything—and when they did, they'd always tossed it back in the pond—but they'd shared their dreams here, sketching futures neither of them ever saw, whiling away the summer days before school gobbled them up again for another year.

There weren't many leaves left on the old weeper now, but the whippy branches formed enough of a curtain to conceal Ben inside.

In *his* day, an ambitious boy had to straddle the trunk and shimmy up those first precarious six feet, pressing his skin against the coarse bark, always risking a dip in the cold green water if he lost his grip. But somewhere along the line, a much smarter kid had nailed a series of wooden slats to the trunk, neatly spacing them into ladder rungs spanning all the way up to the bench.

A voice in Ben's head said, *Put it out of your mind.*

And he slipped off his loafers and started climbing. Near the top, his big toe curled into a painful cramp and he damn near went ass-over-teakettle into the drink— but he caught himself in time, hunkering down to clutch the trunk as he had as a boy. When the cramp let up, he finished the climb, getting his legs angled around so his stocking feet dangled over the pond. He felt lightheaded looking down into that dark soup—the surface of which seemed a lot closer now than it had when he was a boy—and he closed his eyes until the feeling passed. When he looked down again, he saw the striped head of a painted turtle breaking the surface—

"Benjamin Hunter, have you lost your *mind*?"

Ben turned to the familiar voice and saw another head, this one poking through the willow branches, Melanie looking up at him goggle-eyed now, one slender hand extended as if to catch him should he fall.

He smiled, thinking, *She cares*, and said, "Why don't you kick off those sensible shoes and join me?"

She said, "You really *have* lost your mind," and stepped into the dappled pocket of shade. "At my age." But she was slipping out of her Hush Puppies now, gazing up at him with those vexingly playful eyes, showing him the smile that had slain him so many years ago and drenched him in longing now.

She set her shoes next to his on the bald ground and started climbing. Halfway up, she shot him a scolding glance, saying, "These are my favorite dress pants, Ben Hunter. If I get one *speck* of dirt on them, I'll be sending you the dry-cleaning bill."

"Fair enough," Ben said, impressed by her agility as she settled in next to him on the natural bench, the warmth of her hip sending a current of excitement through his body. She wiggled a bit now, trying to find the best spot, saying her old backside was bony and she wasn't sure how long she could sit up here. Ben told her to quit whining and Melanie gave him a companionable swat.

Facing her now, he said, "I'm glad you came. Have you been talking to Roxanne?"

"Yes, just this morning. She's settling in nicely. She sounds excited, but I can tell she's homesick."

"I got that feeling, too. Quinn and Wilder were over last night when she called and we got her on speaker phone. Quinn was trying out some of his new jokes on her, but they were so rude I had to kick the bum out."

"Did she laugh?"

"Like a lunatic."

"Tell me one."

"Jeez, Mel, I don't know. Off-color doesn't even begin to describe them."

She swatted him again. "You've seen me naked. Now *tell* me."

Ben grinned, his mind serving up a luminous image of them as teenagers, naked as the day they were born, propped sideways across Melanie's bed in front of the mirror, taut bodies at the peak of youthful perfection, Melanie's breasts shock-white against the tan of her skin. They'd just had sex, and —

Another swat.

Ben said, "You expect me to concentrate *now*?"

"Focus."

Exhilarated by Melanie's lively mood, Ben skimmed through Quinn's gags in his mind, trying to decide which was the least offensive. Then he said, "I'm not a great joke-teller, but here goes…"

She smiled in anticipation, cornflower eyes locked on his.

"Okay, so this guy's been married to the same woman for fifteen years, and after work one day he's talking about his sex life with his buddies at the bar. So he says, 'I finally got up the nerve to ask her how she'd rate my performance, and you know what she says? I make too much noise when I come. So I ask her what she means, and she tells me it wakes her *up*.'"

Now Ben thought he'd ruined the mood. The gleam in Melanie's eyes had dimmed, and that expectant smile had puckered into a thoughtful rosebud.

Then her shoulders began to shake and Ben realized she was laughing, laughing so hard he thought she was going to topple backward into the pond. Galvanized, he threw an arm around her shoulders, startling her, and now she really *was* falling. By reflex, she grabbed his shirt, and now they were *both* caught in gravity's merciless sway—

Ben's left hand swung out blindly, seized the stump of a sawed-off branch—and they were saved. Because she'd lost her balance first, Melanie ended up angled beneath him, and when he drew her upright they were face to face, noses almost touching. Surprising him, Melanie wrapped her hand around the back of his neck and drew him in until their lips touched.

Now she breathed his name and wet her lips, and Ben kissed her, his questing mouth joining hers, their tongues stirring like tiny, starved animals awakened from a prolonged hibernation. She kept moaning his name—"Oh, Ben, oh, Ben,"—and he felt himself becoming aroused, the depth of her passion in this somehow hallowed place propelling him back across time again, to their first kiss in this very spot a lifetime ago, and his startlement even then that such a sweet, reserved girl could be capable of such unhinged intensity.

But then, as quickly as it began, it was over. She pulled away, pressed a warm hand over his mouth, and fixed him with tear-filmed eyes, the fire in them replaced by what looked like pity.

She said, "I'm so sorry, Ben. I just wanted to...I *needed* to see if I could feel that way again, and I *do*, I really do."

She was moving away from him now, starting down the ladder with that damnable agility, and he knew he couldn't keep up. She was on the ground with her shoes on before he got his leg swung around to straddle the seat, looking at him now with those sad, somehow pitying eyes.

"I can't do this, Ben. Not again. Not at my age."

It was that day at Le Château all over again, and he felt pathetic, ready to beg for another chance. He said, "But Mel—"

"Ben, please. Just let it go."

She was heading for the curtain of branches now, about to leave him again, and he said, "Mel, wait." She stopped but didn't turn around. "Where's the harm in this? I still love you. I always have. And judging by what we just shared, you *must* feel the same way."

Now she did turn, her melancholy expression amplified by a rueful smile. "That's always been your problem, Ben. Mistaking sex for love."

The statement threw him and he only stared at her.

She said, "I'm leaving now. I can't see you anymore, Ben. I don't want you to call me, and I don't want you dropping by. This in no way reflects on your relationship with Roxanne. She loves you very much and I would never interfere with that."

She paused, seemed to have more to say...then she was gone, the willow branches closing behind her like a funeral shroud.

Scrambling now, Ben started down the ladder, shouting her name at the top of his lungs. When he hit the ground and turned to retrieve his shoes, Melanie was there, droop-shouldered and expressionless. Ben threw his arms around her, but she stood motionless, arms dangling by her sides.

Taking a step back in his socks, he said, "All right, Mel. I get it. There's little point if we're not in the same place."

The tears were back, brimming on her lids. "It's not that, it's..."

"What *is* it, then. Please tell me. I have to know."

There was gunmetal in her eyes now, that gentle blue as dark as a thunderhead. She said, "You're sick, Ben. And I can't look after you. I won't."

Ben smiled, his heart vaulting out of the mud. "No, no, I'm *fine* now. Didn't Roxanne tell you? I'm on a new medication."

Now her eyes seemed almost black. She said, "It's not working."

Then she was gone.

THIRTEEN

Friday, September 15 – *Constance Bay*

BEN CHECKED HIS WATCH for the tenth time in as many minutes, excitement loose in him like a prancing stallion.

One hour to go.

True, she'd only given him a 'maybe', but every instinct told him she was coming. He'd heard it in her voice when she called last night. The desire.

She's coming.

She'd called to apologize for what she'd said that day under the weeping willow, telling him she'd overreacted, saying maybe they *could* go back to seeing each other casually if he still wanted to, she really did enjoy his company. But she wouldn't promise to join him here for dinner tonight. Just like she wouldn't promise to meet him at the willow tree.

And yet she'd come.

She'd jotted his directions to the cottage, too—another good sign—and said if she *did* come, he'd better behave himself.

She's coming.

He was glad he'd taken Roxanne's advice and waited for Melanie to make the next move, as excruciating as that had been. Roxanne had called him that same night, saying Gram had told her what happened.

"But I can tell she cares about you, Ben. And I know she feels terrible about some of the things she said, which all but guarantees she'll get in touch with you. She can't bear that kind of guilt for long without apologizing. She asked me to do it for her, but I refused. Told her she'd have to do it herself."

"Wow. Looks like you've got a patch of that Anderson grit in you, too."

Roxanne laughed. "I learned from the best. So hang in there, okay? She'll be in touch. You may not like what she has to say, but at least it'll give you an opening."

"She said I'm sick, Roxanne. She said the pills aren't working."

"I talked to her about that, too." She hesitated. "How *have* you been doing, Ben?"

"I'm right as rain. Haven't had a spell in weeks."

Another hesitation. "Are you really the best judge?"

"I hear what you're saying. But the boys tell me I'm peachy—I *know*, that's like an endorsement from two of the Three Stooges—but I've been following up with Doctor Skeen, and he says I'm a hundred percent."

"That's great news, Ben. Look, I've gotta go. I'm late for class. But trust me on this, okay? *Don't* call her. She'll come around. And I'll be working on her behind the scenes."

"I'll do my best."

"You'd better. And whatever you do, do *not* spring that engagement ring on her."

He'd chuckled at that. "You have no idea how charming I can be."

"No one on the *planet* is that charming. Trust me. If you try that, you'll never see her again."

"Okay, sweetheart. Duly noted."

And sure enough—last night—Melanie had called.

* * *

Restless now, Ben took another pass through the cottage, checking to make sure everything was just right. Dinner thawing in the microwave: Stouffer's Chicken in Barbeque Sauce, his favorite. A pricey Pinot Noir chilling in the fridge. Table set for two by the window overlooking the river. Dinner candles ready for the flame. Radio tuned to a commercial-free classical station, perfect for the atmosphere he was trying to create. A crackling fire in the open hearth, almost too hot for the main floor. He'd have to remember to crack a window before she got here.

He went upstairs next, to the master bedroom, the double bed neatly made. He wished he had chocolates for the pillows, like in the best hotels, a whimsical touch he always enjoyed. More candles up here, scented ones, arranged in threes on the nightstands. A white terry-cloth bathrobe for each of them—just in case—hanging from curved brass hooks on the closet door.

He grinned, thinking, *No harm in hoping*, the prospect of intimacy, however remote, making him feel like a kid again. It brought to mind the first time they'd had sex, both of them virgins, Melanie leading him upstairs by the hand, saying, "I swear, Benjamin Hunter, if I waited for you to make the first move, I'd end up an old maid." That first time hadn't lasted very long—less than a ten-count, if memory served—Santana's "Soul Sacrifice" blaring on a tinny cassette player by the bed, the fever-ish Latin rhythms barely matching the urgency he'd felt. He'd gotten the hang of it eventually, though, learning to rein in that feverish rush and bring the same exquisite pleasure to his lover.

Smiling at the memory, Ben rearranged the throw pil-lows a few times, then sniffed the air, deciding it was still a bit musty up here. He considered lighting one of the scented candles, then thought better of it. If he burned the place down while they were having dinner, it'd put a serious damper on the evening. He sprayed the room with *Febreze* instead. Hawaiian Aloha. An ap-propriate scent for what he had planned.

Before leaving, he appraised the room from the doorway, thinking, *Perfect*. Thinking, *But God, it's hot up here*. He was filmed in sweat now, a dull ache in his chest. *Damn it*. He tried the only window and found it painted shut.

He checked his watch on the way downstairs, wondering if he had time for another shower.

"Scratch that. What if she shows up early and you don't hear her knock?"

Talking to yourself now, Benjamin? His father's voice, at once reproachful and amused.

He filled the kitchen sink with cold water and dunked his face, scrubbing it with both hands. It'd have to do.

Feeling refreshed, he dried off with a fistful of paper towels and checked his watch again.

Forty minutes to go.

Time to rehearse his speech.

He returned to the living area and sat in his place at the dinner table. The chair on the right. He'd have to remember that or his plan would be blown before he got started. Earlier, he'd tucked the engagement diamond and the long-outdated tickets to Hawaii in a plastic baggie and scotch-taped it to the underside of the table. The plan was to keep the conversation light during dinner, then secretly dig the ring out of the baggie, take her hand in the candlelight and say his piece. If she went for it, he'd slip the ring on her finger, pull out the plane tickets and hand them over—with a promise to buy new ones as soon as they'd set a date.

He was really sweating now, nerves taut as piano wire, but he wanted to get through the speech a few more times before she got here. What he didn't want was to end up stammering like a schoolboy when he made his bid.

He took a deep breath. Held it. Let it out.

Then, facing the vacant chair opposite, he said, "Mel, I realize this is sudden—"

Jesus, boy, look at yourself. His father's voice again. *Talking to a goddamn chair.*

Ben said, "You're right," to the empty room and stood. There was a porcelain opera mask on the wall over the loveseat, bone-white with candy-apple lips and almond-shaped eyeholes. Ben took it down and scotch-taped it to the backrest of Melanie's chair. He stepped away to inspect his work, and decided it needed something more.

He found a mop in the utility closet by the stove, the old-fashioned kind with a wooden handle and stringy gray dreadlocks. Amused now, he wedged the handle between the spindles of Melanie's chairback, then hung the mask where the face should be and sat again in his spot. A little tall for Mel, but it'd have to do.

Facing it now, he said, "Melanie, I realize this is sudden..."

* * *

Though Ben's speech wasn't long, it *was* direct and intense, and it took him several dry-mouthed attempts before he felt he had it down. Stumbling through it the first few times, he'd barely been able to look his Melanie-mannequin in the eyeholes, never mind how poorly he might have done had she been sitting there in person. But gradually, it all seemed to come together, with just the right blend of courage and humility to convey his sincerity.

He checked his watch again, startled to discover the appointed hour had come and gone. Mel was already a half-hour late.

Ben got to his feet, hip joints punishing him for the prolonged inactivity. The hearth fire had diminished to a bed of coals, but the room was hotter than ever. He thought, *I've got to remember to crack a window in here*, but the thought was swamped by a wave of melancholy, a louder voice telling him his guest of honor wasn't coming.

He shuffled to the foyer and pressed his forehead to the sidelight, cupping his hands to peer through thin porch light into the darkness beyond.

Nothing moving out there. No headlights picking their way up the hill from the cottage road.

She's not coming.

His cell phone rang, startling him, and Ben felt his heart rise like a sprung blind. It was Melanie, it *had* to be, calling to say she was running late.

He almost dropped the phone bringing it to his ear.

"Mel?"

"You mean she's not there yet?"

It was Quinn.

Ben said, "She's probably just running late."

"You should call her. Maybe she's lost."

"I told her to call *me* if she got lost and I'd talk her the rest of the way in." He glanced at the power bars on his phone. "Look, Ed, I appreciate you driving me up here this morning, and I look forward to seeing you guys for the barbeque on Sunday. But my phone's almost dead and I forgot the charger at home."

"Okay, buddy, I'm off. Are you *sure* you want me to drag Wilder up there on Sunday? You know what he's like around free food."

"Bring him, don't bring him. Either way, I've gotta go."

"Okay, buddy. Good luck tonight. I hope you get your wick wet."

Ben said, "Asshole," and hung up.

* * *

He stood watch by the sidelight for a time, thoughts drifting with the clouds out there, silvery spindles gliding past the moon like longboats. It occurred to him to rehearse the speech again, in defiance of the cynical voice that continued to insist she wasn't coming (a glance at his watch all but confirmed it), but he wasn't ready to go down that road just yet.

His bladder shrilled at him now, and he headed for the bathroom to relieve himself, unclasping his belt as he climbed the stairs. He sat on the john, struggling at first to get his plumbing started...then it came in a satisfying stream. He sighed —

And thought he heard something.

Just the cottage settling, he decided, dabbing himself dry with toilet paper. He got his pants done up, gave his fingers a rinse—and heard it again.

A crunch of gravel outside?

Ben dried his hands and returned to the foyer. He peered through the sidelight again, but apart from a bulking thunderhead screening the moon out there now, the scene was unchanged. No car in the driveway. No Melanie on the stoop.

Accepting the obvious, he switched off the exterior light. She was two hours late. No sense kidding himself any longer.

She isn't coming.

Outside, thunder grumbled.

And Ben thought, *What if she really is lost?*

He decided to call her on the cell Roxanne had given her before leaving for Dalhousie. "It's my old iPhone," she told him. "I thought it might come in handy some-day, you know, in case of emergency. I made Gram promise to keep it in her purse. You might as well have the number."

Now where did I put that piece of paper?

Then he remembered. The inside pocket of his suit coat. He'd left it on the back of his chair at the dinner table, so he wouldn't forget which seat was his.

Concerned now, he hurried down the hall to the din-ing area.

Melanie was sitting where the mannequin had been, holding a goblet of Pinot Noir. She smiled when their eyes met, candlelight erasing the decades from her face.

Ben stood mute in the middle of the room, the stone hearth baking his back, his jaw unhinged. It was that first day at her locker all over again and he couldn't move a muscle.

Melanie said, "Benjamin Hunter, you give lousy directions."

"Uh..."

"I let myself in, I hope you don't mind. I knocked but nobody came."

"Uh..."

"If you're wondering where your friend is, I put her out on the deck. I don't mean to be rude, but the girl needs a shampoo."

"Uh...you're *here*."

"In the flesh."

"I didn't see your car..."

"I got my friend Barb to drive me. My night vision's not what it used to be."

"Shouldn't we invite her in?"

"Cute. She's gone home."

Ben paused to relish the implications.

Still smiling, Melanie shook her head, saying, "Are you planning on standing there all evening or are you going to come over here and join me?"

Ben hurried to his chair, face cramping from the width of his grin. He took a gulp of the wine Melanie poured for him and felt under the table for the baggie. Then he saw it on the tablecloth next to her hand.

He said, "How did...?"

"Scotch tape let go. And Roxanne ratted you out. I'm assuming the...whatever that was...the *mop* lady, was a prop of some kind?"

Ben said, "I was rehearsing my speech," surprised at how calm he felt now.

Melanie said, "That's what I figured," an antic gleam in her eyes. "Though I fail to see the resemblance."

"I've got a good imagination." He indicated the baggie, candlelight dancing in the modest diamond inside. "So you know all of it?"

"Girls talk, Ben. You should know that by now."

"That little traitor. She'll be getting a stern talking-to over the phone in the morning."

"You'll do no such thing."

He smiled. "That's correct."

"So this speech…"

"Would you like to hear it?"

She said, "I would," and reached into the top of her blouse, plucking out something suspended from the delicate chain around her neck. Concealing the object in her hand, she said, "But I have a few things I'd like to say first."

"Okay." He couldn't believe she was here.

"You broke my heart, Ben. I was crazy about you, but I always had to compete for your attention. I knew your studies were important, and I admired your drive. And God, look at all the wonderful things you've done with your life. All the important things you've accomplished."

"Melanie, I—"

"Please. Let me finish." She was clutching the object in her hand now, squeezing it under her chin. "I wanted a simpler life. Needed it. A nice house in a quiet neighborhood. A vegetable garden in the backyard. A baby or two. And a companion. Over everything else, Ben, a companion. To talk to. To hold onto in the night."

"And I couldn't give you that."

Nodding, she showed him what was in her hand. It was his grandfather's wedding band, the one he'd given her in their teens when he asked her to go steady.

"I kept this in a shoebox at the back of my closet. This and the red rose you gave me at the Sadie Hawkins dance. And the ticket stubs from the Red Skelton show at the Civic Center. Wasn't he just the funniest man? And all of your letters."

Tears stood in her eyes now, and Ben wanted to touch her.

But he waited.

"I met Jamie, my first husband, while you were in Edmonton. He was the exact opposite of you. Reckless. Aggressive. Dangerous." She chuckled and a tear fell. "My mother couldn't stand him. He drove a motorcycle and wore filthy leathers. She thought I'd lost my mind. And I guess I had. After he got me pregnant with Elizabeth, he told me he wanted to 'do the right thing by the kid'—his exact words—and God help me, I married the man.

"Theo was a different story." She was blushing now, but she held his gaze. "In my whole life, Ben, I never again felt the heat I did with you. That unquenchable *passion*. It made me insane. It was like a drug."

Ben thought, *I know exactly what you mean.* He was feeling it now, welling up like lava. It was a dream come true.

Melanie said, "But like any drug that ends in dependency...I *ached* for you when you were away from me. Those long hours you spent at the university, and then later, at the hospital. I was miserable. Just miserable.

"So I traded loneliness for danger. And when danger fled, I found Theo. My companion. A man who wanted the same things I did. And he loved me, Ben, with all his heart. He worked nine-to-five at a hardware store three blocks from the house. When the weather was fine, I'd make lunch for us both and bring it up to the store. I felt safe with him. And when he came home at night, he was *home*."

She rested her hand on top of his. "But it wasn't the same. When I saw you coming up the porch steps with Roxanne that day, I decided on the spot I'd never let you back into my heart.

"But here I am."

"Yes," Ben said. "Here you are."

She placed her free hand over the plastic bag. "I'm not going to marry you, and I'm too damned old for Hawaii. But I am going to spend the night. Why don't we start with that?"

Delighted, shell-shocked, Ben nodded his approval. Unsure how to proceed, he said, "Uh, I've got dinner in the microwave..."

Melanie stood now, pulling him to his feet, saying, "I'm not that kind of hungry."

And repeating an act that propelled him back across the years as effectively as any time machine, she led him upstairs by the hand.

FOURTEEN

Sunday, September 17 – *The Barbeque*

QUINN GUIDED HIS AGING Chevy Cruze along the gravel cottage road at half the speed limit, checking each overgrown entryway for the sign Ben had said to watch out for: *Hunter's Hollow*. Wilder, hunched in the shotgun seat, was supposed to be watching for the sign, but he was too busy screwing with the radio and complaining about every little thing.

The car hit a pothole now and Wilder bumped his head on the dash. Cursing, he switched the radio off. "Nothing but Country anyway." He touched his forehead, then checked his fingers for blood. "Why in the name of Christ would you own such a runty little shit-box, man? Look at you. Your big melon barely fits in here."

Quinn chuckled. "Room for your ass and a gallon of gas. It was my wife's car."

"Well, you should junk it and buy a Humvee. Show a little pride."

"Who can afford a vehicle like that? And I drive what, once a month?" He pulled up next to a homemade sign partially obscured by goldenrod, but it said, *The Gallaghers*. He rechecked the map Ben had drawn. "Shit, it's gotta be around here someplace."

"Didn't you drive the man two days ago?"

"Yeah, but he *knows* where the friggin' place is."

Wilder said, "And you didn't pay attention." He pointed through the windscreen. "Next one up on the left."

The asshole was right.

Quinn said, "You been here before?"

"No, but I still have my eyesight." He rubbed his forehead again. "Goddamn, that's gonna raise a goose egg."

Continuing to idle under the baking sun, Quinn said, "I hope it worked out between him and Mel. Poor bastard's still head-over-heels."

"If you took your foot off the brake, maybe we could find out."

Ignoring Wilder now, Quinn made the left-hand turn, entering a sun-dappled tunnel of birch and poplar, the gravel lane rutted from neglect.

They came to the foot of a steep rise and Wilder said, "According to the map, he should be right at the top of this hill. I hope the son of a bitch has HP Sauce. I meant to bring a bottle and forgot it on the counter."

Lumbering up this last stretch of road, Quinn said, "Or confused it with a beer and chugged it."

"Funny."

They crested the hill and came to a stop, both men silent now, taking in the view.

Grinning, Quinn said, "Look at this place. It's paradise up here."

"Notice anything else?"

"What do you mean?"

"No car."

Quinn thought, *Shit*, and felt his grin fall away.

Wilder said, "No sweet nooky for Benji," and patted the bulge in his pocket. "Good thing I brought combustibles. If I gotta look at long faces all day, I'm gonna need to be high."

"You're always high. Maybe they went for a drive. Ben said there's a grocery store nearby. Maybe they went for HP Sauce. You're always so negative."

"Well, park this Dinky Toy and let's see what's up."

* * *

Knocking hard on the front door for the third time, Quinn said, "See? No one's here. Dimes to doughnuts they went to the store."

"Or the dozy bugger cabbed home with his tail between his legs and neglected to tell us. Jesus *Christ*, it's hot out here."

Realizing Wilder had a point, Quinn knocked again, then cocked an ear to the door, listening into a silence marred only by the distant rattle of a chainsaw.

Wilder said, "Screw this," and turned the knob. The door swung open onto a blast of dry heat more stifling than outside. Stepping into the foyer, Wilder said, "No A/C in here?"

Quinn watched him stride across the main floor and open the deck door, admitting a gentle river breeze.

Now the dummy hollered, "Anybody home?" and Quinn shushed him, saying, "Hey, man, keep it down. If Melanie stood him up, he might still be sleeping."

"It's one in the afternoon," Wilder said, checking the fridge now, saying, "No *beer*? What kind of Sunday-school barbeque are we in for here today?"

Quinn said, "Like you've never slept in." He glanced into the stairwell. "I'll go upstairs and see if he's there. And keep it down, will you? If he's still asleep, we'll smoke a bowl and wait for him on the deck."

"Good idea. I'll see you out there."

Quinn started into the stairwell, wincing every time a riser creaked under his weight. If Mel *had* stood Ben up, he was going to need a sympathetic ear—which made Quinn wish he'd left that mocking dickhead Wilder at home.

There was a landing about a dozen steps up, then a ninety-degree turn followed by another six steps. At the top of the second flight, Quinn glanced in both directions along a tiled hallway, seeing a bathroom to his right and what looked like a couple of bedrooms to his left.

No one in the bathroom. No one in the first bedroom, either. A glance from the hallway had him convinced the second bedroom was deserted as well, the drawn curtains admitting only a pale sliver of light.

Then his eyes adjusted and settled on the bed.

Ben lay on his side in there, cast in a stillness too profound for sleep. His topmost arm lay slung across the handle of a mop with a porcelain opera mask tangled in its ratty strands. Ben's eyes were open, fixed on that ghostly mask.

Swallowing hard, Quinn padded into the room, drawn by a tiny, star-shaped reflection on Ben's hand... an engagement diamond, Quinn realized, snugged against the first knuckle of his ring finger.

"Aw, Benji."

Wanting to be certain, Quinn checked for a pulse—there was none—and thought he saw a glint in his friend's eyes, eyes that seemed to track him in the chancy light. Instead of the dull black gaze of the dead, Quinn believed he saw an eerie contentment in those eyes, as if with his final breath, his old pal had beheld the face of God.

Overcome by a sense of trespass now, Quinn backed out of the room and crept into the stairwell, hackles bristling as the creep became a dash and he burst out the front door to throw up in the hedge.

* * *

Roxanne flew home for the memorial service, hosted by the chapel and presided over by the diminutive Sister Mary Grace. In accordance with Ben's wishes, his ashes were secured in a plain oak box Ely had built for him when he was a kid. With Gram's help, Roxanne enshrined it on a bed of petals surrounded by elaborate flower arrangements, many of which had been sent by prominent people: the mayor; the prime minister; the billionaire Francis Riley and his wife; and Ben's many other friends and colleagues. Quinn had provided an enlarged photo of Ben as a much younger man, dapper in his black graduation togs, Oxford cap tilted at a rakish angle, smile as brilliant as the flash-glare on his framed MD degree.

In the car on the way to the service, Gram told Roxanne she hadn't called Ben yet to apologize, and had no idea he'd been waiting at the cottage. As was her way, she didn't sugarcoat what her response would have been had she known. "I was honest with him, honey. I loved the man once. Loved him like crazy. But that was a long time ago. And he was sick, we both see that now. I couldn't go through that again, Roxanne, watching someone I care about wither away. I hope you understand."

"Of course I do, Gram. I just wish things could have been different."

"Me too, sweetie. Me too."

Several people got up to say a few words, including Ely, Quinn, Wilder, Francis Riley, and the old Russian physicist Ben had told Roxanne about. But it was Gram's brief contribution that affected her most.

Dry-eyed now, the old woman spoke directly to Ben's photo. "This is from Tolkien, old friend. Sweet lover." She cleared her throat and said, 'All that is gold does not glitter, not all those who wander are lost; the old that is strong does not wither, deep roots are not reached by the frost.'

"If God is good, Benjamin Hunter, I'll see you again soon."

* * *

On the day before her return flight to Halifax, Roxanne borrowed Gram's car and drove to Ben's cottage in the rain. His ashes rested next to her on the passenger seat, her right hand breaking contact with the box only infrequently.

She parked at the top of the hill and tucked the box into a plastic bag to protect it from the rain, which had tapered now to a chill September drizzle. She strode to the front of the cottage and chose a spot she knew Ben adored, an enormous shade tree with a lofty view of the river and the forested hills beyond. Sheltered in its lee, she removed the box from the plastic bag and opened the lid, flinching when a gust tugged a wisp of her friend's remains into the air.

She said, "I love you, Ben. Thank you for loving me back."

Reverently, she tilted the box, watching as Ben's ashes blossomed around her, a gust dispersing them in gossamer curtains.

She lingered a while, remembering, then made her way back to the car, autumn thunderheads grumbling at her heels.

ABOUT THE AUTHOR

Sean Costello is the author of nine novels and numerous screenplays. His thriller *Here After* has been optioned to film by David Hackl, director of *Saw V*. Sean's horror novels have drawn comparisons to the works of Stephen King, and his thrillers to those of Elmore Leonard. Sean is currently hard at work on several new writing projects.

To stay up to date on the author's latest projects, sign up for his newsletter at www.seancostello.net.